WICKED RESPITE

An Ivy Morgan Mystery Book Fourteen

LILY HARPER HART

HarperHart Publications

❀ Created with Vellum

One

Jack Harker was a brave man, but he never thought shopping for camping supplies would be on his agenda. It wasn't that he thought of himself as an indoor guy as much as he thought sleeping on the ground was for the young. Despite that, he found himself pushing a huge cart inside an outdoor adventure store as his fiancée Ivy Morgan studied each aisle with great detail.

"Is there such a thing as a heated tent?" he asked.

Slowly, Ivy tracked her eyes to him. "What do you mean?"

"Just what I said. I don't like being cold."

"We could get a space heater and take it with us. We'll have to buy batteries but there are chargers we can get that run off the battery of your truck to charge them, if that's what you want."

Jack made a series of popping noises with his lips as he pretended to study the wall of sleeping bags to his right. "Do you think we should do that?"

Ivy managed to keep her face placid even though it was a chore. Jack was a city boy, she reminded herself. He grew up in the rough neighborhoods surrounding Detroit. No one camped in that area ... at least not at a place that didn't feature a cartoon bear on the brochures.

"Maybe we should do something else," she hedged, wrapping her hand around his wrist and carefully pulling him away from the sleeping bags. "We could go to a hotel for a weekend or something. That's easier and still a chance for us to get away."

Jack's gaze was withering as he pinned her with a dark look. "No. I said we were going camping."

"Yes, but ... ." Ivy was at a loss. She loved Jack beyond reason, but she had things to say. Those things were unlikely to go over well if she didn't measure her response and take Jack's feelings into consideration.

Jack knew Ivy better than anyone. They'd been introduced a little more than a year ago. In that time, however, they'd completely fallen head-over-heels for one another. Their lives were so intertwined from the start that Jack never labored under the delusion they wouldn't end up together. From the start, it seemed they were destined to be each other's forever. He still believed that, despite the conundrum he found himself in now.

"We're going camping." He was firm as he turned back to the sleeping bag display. "I'm perfectly capable of roughing it in the wilderness of the Upper Peninsula. It was a simple question."

Ivy, her long brown hair (which was streaked with hints of pink) hanging over her shoulders in a wavy sheet, tilted her head to the side. "We can get the heater." She wanted him to be comfortable more than anything else. If he was worried about being cold, that would be the source of unneeded stress. "It's a good idea."

The look he shot her was full of annoyance. "You're laughing at me inside, aren't you?"

"No." Ivy immediately started shaking her head. "I'm not. I love you. I would never laugh at you."

She was so earnest Jack took pity on her. "Ivy, I love you, too. I've never doubted you love me. Your head is full of laughter, though. You might as well admit it because we both know it's true. You're not fooling anybody."

Ivy worked her lower jaw as she debated her options. Finally, she blew out a sigh. "Okay, here's the thing: The tent we've got is relatively big, but it's also warm. I know this because I helped pick it out. It's thermal. We're not going to freeze to death."

"This is earlier in the season from last year, though," he pointed out. "The afternoons are fairly warm now, but the nights are still cool. Plus, we're driving two hours up north. I mean ... we're going to be in the official north of the north. That means it's going to be colder."

Ivy had to bite the inside of her cheek to keep from laughing. Jack was the sort of man who liked to plan things out to the best of his ability. She, on the other hand, was more willing to fly by the seat of her pants and manage the outcome as it occurred. They were very different in that respect and yet she believed they were perfectly suited for one another. Her heart broke out in song whenever she caught sight of him. Her skin hummed when he drew near. It was as if their souls recognized one another from the start, she often mused. Once meeting, they both knew they couldn't make it without one another. It was folly to ever try.

"Hey." Jack snapped his fingers in front of her face and frowned. "Where was your head? I'm having a serious conversation with you. I don't want to freeze to death ... and it's as if I can see you rolling your eyes even when I'm not looking at you."

Ivy heaved out a sigh. It was obvious he was about to melt down because he thought she was internally laughing at his lack of outdoor acumen. "Jack, we're not going to freeze to death." Gently, she reached out and linked her fingers with his. "Do you think I would risk that? We have two thermal sleeping bags. We're going to zip them together like before. We'll be sharing warmth so it will be hotter than you think."

She didn't realize that she'd let a double entendre fly until she saw the wicked intent in his eyes. "Oh, geez." She made a face. "Your mind just went to a dirty place, didn't it?"

"You have no idea." Jack's smile widened as he slid an arm around her waist and tugged her to him. "Basically you're saying that our chemistry is combustible and we'll be sweating no matter how cold it is."

"I didn't say that. Not even remotely."

"Funny, that's what I heard."

"That's because you're a pervert." Even though she was faking annoyance with him, she couldn't hold on to one iota of faux anger as she snuggled close and pressed her lips to his strong jaw. "I love you,

Jack." The words escaped long before she realized she was going to utter them. Before he came into her life, Ivy was the sort of person who flew off the handle when she was angry but thought long and hard about the things she was going to say when she was trapped in the moment. With Jack, she could say whatever she wanted and not live in fear. He never held it against her.

He tilted her head back so he could stare into the sea blue of her eyes. "I love you, too, honey." He lowered his lips to hers and gave her a smoldering kiss. It was so hot, Ivy's eyes rolled back in her head and she momentarily forgot where they were.

Then she heard whispering.

When they pulled apart, Ivy found herself staring at two women in their thirties. They were down the aisle looking at lanterns but didn't bother to hide their interest in what was going on between Ivy and her intended.

"Sorry," Ivy offered lamely, wiping the corners of her mouth. "We just got distracted."

Neither woman smiled.

"This is a family store," one of them pointed out. She was a brunette with a bob haircut and some rather unattractive blunt bangs that made her face look a little too square. "This is not a sex store."

Ivy's contrition disappeared. "We weren't having sex. Get over yourselves."

"It was close enough," the second woman shot back. "I mean ... this is Michigan, not Vegas. It was almost pornographic."

"Oh, geez." Ivy made an exaggerated face. "I can't even ... ."

Jack moved his hand to her back and slowly rubbed as he regarded the women. "We weren't doing anything," he said finally. "Stop staring and focus on doing ... whatever else it is that you're doing. It would probably be best if you stay out of our business. We'll gladly do the same for you."

"Or perhaps we should call the police," the first woman countered, her eyes flashing. "I'm sure they would be interested to know what you were doing just now."

"I think that's a fabulous idea," Jack agreed without hesitation.

"Since I myself am a police officer, I'm looking forward to that conversation."

Ivy arched an eyebrow as she waited to see how the women would respond. After exchanging obvious eye rolls, they turned the corner and disappeared down the next aisle. Annoyance flashed through Jack's eyes before he slid them to Ivy.

"I think you need to learn to keep your hands off me in public, honey," he said after a beat. "You just offended those women."

Ivy snorted, genuinely amused. "And somehow I can't make myself care."

"Me either." He smacked a loud kiss against her lips and then propelled the cart down the aisle. "Okay, if we don't need a tent or sleeping bags, what else do we need?"

"Our first camping trip was a trial run of sorts," Ivy explained, her mind briefly traveling back to one of the first trips she took with Jack. "That was sort of camping light. This is going to be a more serious effort."

"Does that mean we'll be hunting and killing our own food?" He asked the question with a straight face ... but just barely.

"No, it doesn't. We need some cooking utensils, though. We need a good cooler. The one I have is really old and it's picked up a smell. Not a good smell either, mind you."

"I think that sounds doable." He linked his fingers with hers as they turned the corner. The women were back — they'd positioned themselves down two aisles and were pretending to stare at air mattresses — but Jack knew without a shadow of a doubt what they were really doing. "I think they're jealous," he whispered close to Ivy's ear, sending a chill up her spine as his voice vibrated against the sensitive ridge of her ear. "Should we give them another show? I think they're hot for me and that's why they're hanging around."

"I think we should just ignore them. It will irritate them more than if we said something ... or started fornicating in one of the aisles. Trust me."

"Let's not be hasty." Jack's expression was flirty. "Tell me more about this idea you have for fornicating in the aisles."

"Ha, ha, ha." Ivy rolled her eyes as she moved down the next aisle.

"Okay, here's the stuff I'm talking about. We need cooking utensils, either one big cooler or two smaller ones, and a bunch of these ice packs."

Jack immediately forgot about the judgmental women and widened his eyes when he saw the things Ivy gestured toward. "That's a lot of stuff. I don't even know what we should need. How about I leave it to you to decide and I'll just pay the bill? I think that sounds like a plan."

Ivy poked his side. "You said you wanted to learn."

"I do want to learn. It's just ... this is a lot of stuff."

"We're going to have kids one day," she reminded him. "The whole reason you wanted to learn to camp was so we could go on family vacations with little ones one day."

"That's not the *whole* reason," he argued, his hand absently moving to her back as she started looking at coolers. "I knew you liked camping. I wanted you to be happy."

She stilled. "Is that the only reason we're doing this? If so, we can pick another activity. I love camping, but I don't want you to be miserable."

He wanted to smack himself in the head for saying something so stupid. Ivy had a giving soul. She would gladly subvert her needs for his if she thought it was the best thing for him. He recognized that in her because he was willing to do the same when the roles were reversed.

"How about we stop trying to do what we think will make the other happy and instead focus on what's good for both of us?" he challenged, choosing his words carefully. "You love camping. I love you. I want to give camping a shot. I don't think our first trip counts because it was such a mess."

Ivy thought back to the trip in question and smirked. "You mean because one of your old friends died and another was responsible? The whole week was spent investigating a murder."

"That's exactly what I mean." Jack's expression was grim. "I want an actual vacation. I want us to spend quiet time together, to hike ... and to do whatever people do under the stars."

Her lips curved. "As I seem to recall, you liked the camping nookie just fine. It was the other stuff you didn't like."

He flicked his eyes to her, his heart filling with love as he thought back on the shared moments that had cemented their relationship. "The camping nookie was awesome," he agreed. "I liked looking at the stars ... and your face under the stars.

"We've had a busy couple of months," he reminded her. "Between old witches in the woods ... and reality shows ... and a teenage girl killing her own mother ... we haven't had a lot of time just for ourselves. That's what this trip is for."

Ivy lifted her finger and ran it down Jack's cheek. He had a strong face and it was serious now. "Okay. You have to help with the decisions, though. I can't do this entirely by myself. This is something we're supposed to be doing together."

"Then we'll do it together." Jack was calm and collected as he turned back to the cooking utensils. "For starters, I recommend two smaller coolers rather than one big one. They'll be easier to carry and arrange in the back of the truck."

Ivy brightened considerably. "See. Right there." She jabbed a playful finger into his chest. "Now you're thinking. This is going to be a great camping trip."

"It is," Jack agreed. "Even if it rains every single day and it's just you and me alone in a tent, it's going to be the best time of my life simply because we're together."

Ivy's heart rolled at his earnest expression. It was no wonder that it had been him practically since the moment they met. They somehow fit together as if they were always meant to be a unit. "Let's finish up our shopping and head home. We need to put together a packing list. We're out of here in a day and a half."

"I love that you're so efficient." He slipped his arm around her waist and pressed a kiss to her temple before shuffling over to the coolers. "I think we should get two different colors in case there's a reason we need to separate food items."

"Good idea." Ivy beamed at him. She was starting to enjoy herself. "I happen to like the blue and purple."

"Blue and purple it is. What's next?"

"Cooking utensils."

"I live for shopping for cooking utensils."

Ivy snickered. "That's laying it on a bit thick."

"I knew that the second I said it."

JACK'S TRUCK WAS PACKED WITH new items when the couple landed at the cottage they shared in the woods outside Shadow Lake, a small town in Northern Lower Michigan. The hamlet had been a place for Jack to escape when he was running from his past. Ivy had always lived there, ultimately buying the cottage from her parents when they moved to another place in the same area, and the town was her solace. Together, they'd taken Ivy's childhood home and turned it into their future. In two months, they would be married ... and then a whole new adventure would begin.

To Ivy's utter surprise, her brother Max's truck was in the driveway when they landed. "I wonder what he's doing here."

"I'm sure he's looking for food," Jack replied as he killed the engine and pocketed the keys. "I think he eats frozen dinners when you're not cooking for him."

"No, he has a new girlfriend," Ivy reminded him. "I bet she's cooking dinners for him these days ... even though he seems reticent to let us meet her."

"I met her very briefly at that farmers' market last weekend."

"Yes, when I somehow managed to miss her." Ivy's expression darkened. "I still maintain Max slunk off when he realized we were there because he wanted to hide her from me. There's no other explanation."

"You don't think they simply could've been done and left?" Jack was amused despite himself.

"No. He's hiding her from me. He's afraid I won't like her ... which means there's clearly something wrong with her."

Max and Ivy were as tight as brother-and-sister duos were allowed to be without raising some eyebrows. Jack was aware of that before he got involved with his pink-haired siren. That didn't mean the logistics of their sibling relationship didn't occasionally grate on him. Ivy and Max had a unique way of interacting and it wasn't always comfortable.

"Well, I happen to think she's a perfectly nice woman," Jack countered. "She was pleasant — maybe a little nervous — and she got along great with Max. I think you're going to like her."

"That is if I ever meet her."

"There is that." Jack was all smiles when he exited the truck and found Max descending the front walk. The elder Morgan sibling happily shook Jack's hand in greeting before sliding his eyes to his sister.

"Do I even want to know where you guys have been?" he asked, wrinkling his forehead. "I mean … Ivy looks all glow-y. That usually means you guys have been doing something dirty."

"Unless you count shopping for camping supplies as dirty, we've been angels," Jack countered, pointing himself toward the back of the truck. "I think your sister bought out the store."

"She's always been a big fan of camping supplies," Max agreed, licking his lips. "It's weird that you were just out shopping for your trip because that's kind of why I'm here. I want to talk to you about it."

Ivy sensed trouble. "Dad can still watch the nursery, right?" She owned her own plant nursery, which happened to bump up against the cottage property, and her father worked for her in the summers because he enjoyed talking to the customers and was thrilled with the business Ivy had built for herself.

"Please." Max made a dismissive gesture. "Dad is so excited to be in charge for several days that he's considering making all your employees refer to him as Boss Man Michael. No, seriously. I heard him telling Mom that."

Ivy smirked at the notion. "They'll probably think that's funny. I don't think it's a big deal."

"Definitely not." Max licked his lips and shifted from one foot to the other, clearly uncomfortable. "The thing is … um … ."

Jack was familiar enough with Max's attitude that he understood when the gregarious man was about to drop a bomb on them. "What did you do? If I have to cancel this trip to keep you out of jail, I'm not going to be a happy camper."

"I didn't do anything," Max said hurriedly. "Er, well, almost nothing. In fact, the thing I did is so minor you guys are going to laugh about it … eventually."

Ivy knew her brother's demeanor so well she couldn't help assuming that he was dragging things out for a particular purpose.

"What did you do? You didn't kill someone, did you? I'm not in the mood to hide a body."

Jack pinned her with an annoyed look. "There's little more that I love as much as murder jokes," he drawled.

Ivy ignored him. "Seriously, Max, what did you do? Just tell us."

"I ... well ... you know Amy, right?"

Ivy's lips curved down. "As a matter of fact, I don't know Amy. You disappeared from the farmers' market before I could meet her. That was convenient, by the way."

Jack shot her a quelling look. He recognized that Max was struggling with something very real. "Just tell us what's wrong. Is she pregnant?"

Ivy's mouth dropped open. "Oh, my ... is she pregnant? Mom is going to rip your head off."

Max made an exaggerated face. "She's not pregnant. Stop looking at me that way. She's not. It's something else."

"Then what is it?" Jack prodded. "You'll feel better when you tell us ... and we'll feel better when we know the truth and can figure out a way to help you."

"Okay. Here it is." Max exhaled heavily. "I was talking to Amy and I mentioned your camping trip. She said she's never been camping and it's something she's always wanted to do. Before I realized what was happening — I mean, it was a total fluke — I told her we were invited to go with the two of you and she's so excited she's already home packing."

Max, perhaps reading the way Jack's expression shifted, increased the distance between himself and his future brother-in-law as he hurried toward his truck. "So ... we're coming with you and we're really looking forward to it. Make sure you buy enough food for four, Ivy. Um ... and thanks."

"Come back here!" Ivy planted her hands on her hips as Max scurried toward his truck. "You are not coming with us. This is a private trip."

"Private," Jack echoed, annoyance rumbling through him. "I have plans for your sister that you're not going to like and I'm not adjusting them. You guys are not invited. I'm sorry if it makes you look stupid."

"We'll be here at seven in the morning the day after tomorrow," Max called out. "I thought we could take separate vehicles because it will allow us to break apart and go to dinner without the other couple whenever the opportunity arises ... or run errands and stuff. Isn't that a great idea? Thanks so much for understanding, guys. I'll see you the day after tomorrow."

"Max!" Ivy was a screechy mess as her brother threw himself into his truck to avoid her tone. "We're not finished. You're not going with us."

He merely waved. "This is going to be the best trip ever. Just you wait."

Two

Jack was still bitter two days later when he checked the rearview mirror to make sure Max was following them as they trucked along the two-lane highway that led to a state park he'd never heard of. Ivy mentioned it was one of her favorites – apparently her parents took her and Max there on a regular basis when they were kids – and Jack was excited to visit thanks to her enthusiasm.

Some of that excitement had died when he realized Ivy had capitulated and allowed her brother to tag along on what was supposed to be their private getaway.

"If you want to yell, you can yell," Ivy offered. Her hair was pulled back in a simple ponytail and her face was devoid of makeup. She'd been watching Jack silently pout for the past two hours – ever since they pulled out of the driveway – and she was essentially at her limit. She would rather fight and get it over with than allow him to wallow.

"I'm not going to yell." His tone was bland, flat.

"Why not?"

"You don't like it when I yell."

"That's not true. I don't like it when you order me around. Occasionally I like it when you yell because it means we'll have a ton of fun making up."

His lips quirked, but he managed to keep his stern expression in place. "I'm not going to yell."

"Are you sure?"

"Actually, I'm not."

Ivy felt triumphant. "Then go ahead and unload on me."

"I'm not doing that if I can help it." Jack kept his eyes on the highway. There was very little traffic and yet he seemed intent on reading every sign, something Ivy found fascinating. Jack was out of his element when it came to the wilderness. The fact that he wanted to do this at all was a testament to the sort of man he was ... and Ivy absolutely adored that man. Er, well, most of the time.

"Jack, you'll feel better if you yell," she prodded. "You need to get it out of your system. I would prefer you yell now rather than erupt when we reach the campsite. I don't want to be dressed down in front of Max and his new girlfriend."

Jack let loose a long sigh. "Ivy, I don't want to dress you down at all. Believe it or not, I'm not a fan of acting like an ogre. It's just ... this was supposed to be private time for the two of us. We're getting married in two months. Do you know what that means?"

Ivy nodded without hesitation. "I do. It means I'm going to be able to introduce you as my husband and then watch the way the other women drool when they realize you're all mine."

He told himself that he wouldn't laugh. It would only encourage her. He couldn't stop himself from smiling, though. "You are impossible to stay angry at."

"I believe that's why we make up so often."

"Probably."

Instinctively, Ivy reached over the console and rested her hand on Jack's thigh. "I'm sorry. I know I said I was going to get rid of him, but when I tried to explain our plans he just went on and on about how Amy has never been camping and he wants to show her a good time. I've never seen him this way about a girl before ... or at least not since he was in high school and couldn't control his hormones. He practically begged."

"At which point you still should've told him no."

"I get that but ... he's my brother. I love him. He's done a lot for me over the years. Before you came along, he was the only one I spent any time with because I couldn't make friends I wasn't related to. He was my best friend."

"He's still your best friend," Jack muttered darkly.

"No, you're my best friend."

He slid his eyes to her. "Oh, really?"

She nodded without hesitation. "You're the one person I always want to spend time with no matter what. You listen to me ... and want what's best for me ... and go out of your way to make sure I'm safe and taken care of. If that's not a best friend, I don't know what is."

"Oh, geez." Jack pinched the bridge of his nose, frustration practically rolling off him in waves. "You know exactly how to get what you want from me, don't you? It's unbelievable."

"Just wait until we have a little girl. She'll have you wrapped around her finger faster than you can say 'daddy, will you buy me a pony' and you'll roll over and show her your belly."

Despite himself, Jack laughed. "You're probably right," he acknowledged. "I just picture a little you pointing to every stuffed animal in the store and me walking out with my arms full."

Ivy relaxed, although only marginally. Jack was finally starting to thaw and she wanted to keep the forward momentum going. "When do you want to have kids? I mean ... we haven't really talked about it much."

"When do you want to have kids?"

"I would like to wait a year or two so we can have some time with just us, but I'm open to talking about it if you want to get a jump on things."

"Actually, I like the idea of waiting a year or two as well. I'm perfectly happy with it being just the two of us for the foreseeable future."

Ivy smiled. "That sounds nice."

"Yes. Unfortunately, your brother will probably move in and we'll become a trio until I'm old and gray."

Ivy's smile slipped. "Can't you please let it go? There's nothing you can do to change it. Max is right behind us. I already told him we have romantic plans and he has to put his tent as far away from ours as possible. He doesn't want to be right on top of us any more than we want him to be. I promise you that."

"Oh, I guarantee I want the distance more than he does."

"Jack." The one word carried a mountain of torment. "We're still going to have a great time. I promise. It's going to be all romance, all of the time. You'll have to pry my lips off you."

Even though he fought the effort, Jack's eyes softened. "I'm going to beat him up the first time he interrupts us. I'm not kidding."

"I think that's more than fair."

He moved his hand so it rested on top of hers. "We're going to have a good time. I promise I won't let my bad attitude ruin anything. It's just ... I had big plans for this trip. We've never been away on our own to just relax. The few trips we've taken have ended up with murder and mayhem following us. Now, granted, your brother isn't a murderer. He is all about the mayhem, though."

"It's going to be fine. He wants to romance Amy as much as you want to romance me. We'll probably never see him."

"That would be a nice change of pace." He hit the turn signal when the sign he was looking for popped into view. "Here it is. This is the right campground, right?"

Ivy's expression turned dreamy. "Yeah. I haven't been here since I was a teenager. I can't tell you how excited I am."

"I'm glad." He squeezed her hand before moving both his hands to the wheel. "Don't bother to shine me on about ignoring your brother, though. I happen to know that you're going to be all up in Amy's business because you're dying to learn more about her."

"That's not true. I plan on minding my own business."

Jack snorted. "Whatever. I've got twenty bucks that says you're peppering her with questions before the end of the night."

"You're on."

AMY JOHNSON WAS BLOND, petite, and obviously nervous as she helped Max unload his truck. The way the campsite was arranged, there were large expanses on either side of the bonfire pit. That allowed the two couples to set up shop a decent distance from one another. Ivy was relieved when she saw the site, and despite Jack's earlier teasing, she immediately tapped Amy to help her unload the kitchen stuff for the center table and fire area. Unfortunately for her, Amy was the nervous sort and opted to help Max instead. Ivy wasn't the type to make rash judgments, but the woman's insistence on brushing her off was agitating.

For his part, Max seemed to be having a good time. He laughed as Amy pulled out the instructions for the tent and sat cross-legged on the ground to read them. "You don't need those. I know exactly what I'm doing when it comes to putting up tents. In fact, I'm the best in the business."

Ivy rolled her eyes as she lifted one of the coolers to the top of the picnic table. There were two – one on either side – and she was glad to realize that not every meal would have to be a group affair. "Please. I was the one who put up both our tents when I was a kid."

"That's because I was lazy, not inefficient," her brother shot back, causing Amy to giggle.

She did that a lot, Ivy noted. She giggled ... and shuffled her feet back and forth ... and constantly glanced over her shoulder to make sure nobody was coming up behind her. She was a pretty woman, slim hips and waist setting off slight shoulders. She had big brown eyes, the sort that reminded Ivy of what a puppy would point in her direction, and she seemed enamored with everything Max did.

"What do you think?" Jack asked, sidling up to Ivy and sliding his arm around her shoulders. He'd managed to remove everything from the truck and was now ready to set up their home away from home.

"I think I love you." It was an automatic answer but that didn't mean Ivy didn't mean it.

Jack rolled his eyes. "So sweet." He dropped his arm and lightly pinched her behind, causing her to squeal. "I was talking about your brother's new girlfriend. Do you approve?"

That question wasn't as easy to answer as Ivy would've liked. "I don't know. She seems really ... nervous."

"Do you blame her?"

"Yeah. I'm a delight. She should want to spend all her time getting to know me."

Jack barked out a laugh as he shook his head and turned toward their tent. "You are an absolute delight. I'll fight whomever says otherwise to the death."

Ivy heard something in his words that he didn't say aloud. "But?" she prodded.

"But you have a big personality," he replied without hesitation. "Your brother also has a big personality. She's clearly attracted to that. I'm sure she has her own personality buried under all those giggles. It's not always easy to warm up to people at the drop of a hat, though. You need to give her some time."

Instead of agreeing, Ivy jabbed her finger in his ribs. "I think you're saying that I'm a loudmouth."

"I'm saying that amongst the litany of wonderful traits you have, one of them might be the tendency to take over a room." Jack's smile didn't budge as he grabbed the canvas bag carrying their tent from the ground. "That drew me to you. It was as if you were the only person in the world when we were close to one another. Amy might need a few hours or so to come to grips with that."

Ivy was convinced that was a dig, but she couldn't quite work out how she could pick a fight with him over it. Instead, she took the bag from him. "I'm putting up the tent. I remember what happened last time when you tried it."

"I believe we ended up working together to put up the tent last time, and that's what I want to do this time. I don't want you doing all the work. We're a team."

Even though she wanted to remain petulant, she melted a bit. "We are a team. We're the best team in the world. I think we're always going to be this great of a team. How about you?"

"I happen to agree. Now ... give me a kiss."

"Why?"

"Because I need it."

She rolled her eyes, but it was only for form's sake as she pressed her lips to the corner of his mouth. He returned the kiss with gusto, which earned a gagging noise from Max across the way. Jack jabbed a derogatory finger in his future brother-in-law's direction.

"I wouldn't push me if I were you," he warned, his eyes never leaving Ivy's face. "Just stay on your side of the campsite and everything will be fine."

Max kicked his heels together and offered up a saucy salute. "Yes, sir."

AS JACK AND IVY WENT TO WORK on their tent, Max turned his full attention to Amy. She was eager to help and intent on learning the ropes when it came to camping etiquette. It was obvious she was nervous, though, and he wanted more than anything to make her feel comfortable.

From the first moment he saw her several weeks before – she worked at a bar he frequented and he asked her out four times before she reluctantly agreed, something that caused them to laugh when they looked back on the event – he'd been drawn to her. He didn't even know it was possible to feel an instant connection to a person ... at least not like this.

Oh, he'd listen to his sister and Jack wax poetic on how the atmosphere practically crackled the first time they met. He knew while they didn't exactly believe in love at first sight, they did believe something snapped together that first day. He thought they were full of it until he met Amy. Now he understood.

She wasn't the type he normally went for. He typically liked a woman who commanded every eye in a particular establishment be on her. Amy was quiet and demure, though. She listened well and laughed a lot. She didn't open up much, though, and that was wearing on him. That was one of the reasons he insisted on camping with Ivy and Jack. He thought if anything could draw Amy out, it was seeing him interact with his sister. Ivy had a way with people – even though she didn't see it no matter how hard she looked – and she inspired trust. He hoped Ivy would be able to work her magic on Amy and help the woman to relax a bit.

If he had one complaint, that would be it. Max wanted Amy to trust him implicitly. It seemed that was something she was still working on.

"What are you thinking about?" Amy asked as she inserted metal beams into the canvas harnesses and helped Max pull the tent to a standing position. "Are you sorry we came?"

"Absolutely not." Max was firm as he shook his head. "I want to be here ... and there's no one I would rather be with." Amy was a full foot shorter than him so he had to lean over to kiss her. He didn't mind. In fact, he found her diminutive size to be alluring. It allowed him to sweep her up in his arms on a regular basis. She was so small that he could place her on his lap, wrap himself around her, and she practically melted into him.

Amy's smile was so wide it almost swallowed her entire face when they separated. "This was a good idea."

"Yeah?" Max arched an eyebrow. "I'm glad you think so."

"I'm not sure your sister thinks so." Amy's gaze was pointed when it landed on an arguing Jack and Ivy. They appeared to be having a disagreement over exactly where to put their tent. "I think she wishes we would've stayed behind."

"That's not true." Max immediately started shaking his head. "Ivy is glad you're here. She told me that herself. She wants to get to know you."

"She's kind of ... intimidating," Amy admitted, chewing on her bottom lip. "She's one of those women whom everybody wants to look at ... or be."

Max furrowed his brow, confused. "What do you mean?"

"Look at her. She's comfortable being who she is and doesn't care what anyone thinks." Amy helplessly gestured toward the other woman. "I've never been brave enough to be myself in front of a roomful of people."

Max found the statement odd. "I don't understand. I ... what do you mean?"

"Just that ... look at her hair. I absolutely love it. I would love to try something wild like that."

"You mean the pink?"

"Yeah."

"Well, I believe she does it herself. If you want to try some streaks, I'm sure she'd be willing to help you. She's good at stuff like that."

"And her boyfriend? You said he's a police officer, right?"

"Fiancé," Max corrected. "They're getting married in two months. They won't let anyone forget it either. They're all gooey and in love when they look at each other. It's enough to give you a toothache."

Amy was taken aback. "Is there something wrong with that?"

"Absolutely not. It's just ... she's still my baby sister." His expression darkened as he glanced over at Jack and Ivy, who had settled on a location and were steadfastly working on erecting their tent. "It kind of weirds me out to know the dirty stuff he does with her. I can't help it."

Instead of commiserating, Amy snorted and elbowed him in the stomach. "Your sister is a big girl. She's obviously in love. Jack looks at her as if she's the only woman in the world. He obviously adores her ... and would never purposely hurt her. Most brothers would pray for a man like that to take on their sisters."

She had a point, Max internally mused. "He's still a filthy pig sometimes."

Amy giggled, the sound warming Max to his very core. "Let's finish setting up. I want to help your sister with the food when we're done. I think she was put off when I didn't immediately help with the kitchen stuff. Like I said, though, she makes me a little nervous."

"You'll get used to her. In a few days, you'll hardly remember that you were afraid of her."

"I doubt that."

Max doubted it, too, but he was hopeful that it would become a self-fulfilling prophecy. "Come on. Let's finish this tent and move in. I have something I want to show you before dinner."

Amy snickered. "Your lips?"

"Amongst other things."

Three

Once the tent was put together, Jack made a big show of throwing the sleeping bags inside and then pulling Ivy in after him. The look he shot Max practically dared the man to question him regarding his intentions.

Once it was just the two of them, Max decided it was time to get to know Amy better ... even though he had a few romantic plans of his own.

"So ... you grew up in Minnesota and never went camping?" The notion baffled him. "How did that even come about?"

Amy shrugged, noncommittal. She was busy organizing their bags along the far wall of the tent. "I don't know. My parents simply weren't the camping type. I never got into it."

"You don't talk about your parents much."

"That's because they died a few years ago." She took on a far-off expression as she stared at the cluster of trees on the other side of the site. "Car accident."

"Together?" Max knit his eyebrows. "Are you serious?"

She nodded, rueful. "Yeah. It was horrible. I was living in an apartment on the other side of town. I was about twenty at the time. When the police officer showed up at my doorstep I thought it was a joke at first. A really bad joke, don't get me wrong, but a joke all the same. I just couldn't believe it was happening."

Max's heart went out to her. Instinctively, he moved his hand to her back and slowly rubbed at the slim lines under her shirt. "I'm sorry. I didn't know that. I don't think I ever asked about your parents."

Amy forced a smile for his benefit. "It's not your fault. I didn't ever volunteer the information. It's hard for me to talk about."

"Yeah, but ... I should've asked." Max felt ridiculous for missing something so obvious. "When people start dating, you ask about their family. I never bothered to ask about yours. I'm ... sorry."

Amy took pity on him and squeezed his hand. "You don't need to be sorry, Max. You're the best guy I've ever met. You actually listen when I talk. You have no idea what that means to me."

Max had some idea. He felt the same way when he was talking to her. "I want to be better than that." He offered up the most charming smile in his repertoire. "Tell me about your parents. Were you close with them?"

"Um ... I think it was a normal parent-child relationship. They were good people. I was an only child and they had me late in life. They were both almost forty when I was born and they called me their miracle baby. I thought that was a bit much but ... well ... they seemed to enjoy it so I played along. I used to tease them. When they told me no, I would always say 'is that any way to treat your miracle' and they would laugh. They thought it was funny."

"It sounds funny." Max was at a loss. He had a wide circle of friends. Even though his sister was his best friend, she was hardly his only lifeline in the world and he had a bevy of people to rely on. It sounded to him as if Amy had lost the biggest part of her support team and she'd never managed to replace them moving forward. "No brothers or sister, right? That's what you said."

"I'm an only child. That's why I'm kind of excited to see the way you interact with your sister. I've heard you guys are really close and I want to see how that works."

Max cocked his head to the side. "You've heard?"

"People talk about you around town. I'm new and when we started dating a lot of women approached me to tell stories."

Max's lips curved down. He should've seen that coming. Instead, he didn't even consider it. He could just imagine which women rushed to Amy to give her an earful. "Let me guess ... Maisie Washington and Ava Moffett?"

"How did you know?"

"Let's just say that I'm familiar with their work and leave it at that." Max made a dour face. "What did they say? Wait ... don't answer that." He held up his hand. "I can imagine what they said. For the record, you should know, they've always had attitude where I'm concerned because I refused to date them."

Amy's expression was hard to read. "Oddly enough, they didn't even talk about you all that much. They said you were good looking but to watch out because you have a wandering eye."

Max made a series of protesting noises with his mouth. It took him a full beat to find words. "That is not true. I am not a cheater."

"I don't think they referred to you as a cheater. They simply said that you got bored with women quickly."

Max couldn't exactly argue with that sentiment. The statement wasn't untrue. Still, he didn't want her living in fear that he would suddenly take off and leave one day. He remembered what that fear did to Ivy after she first hooked up with Jack. "That was before I met you." He offered up the most charming smile he could muster. "I think I was doing a lot of searching before. I no longer have to search."

He internally cringed when he heard the words escape his mouth. They were a bit heavy-handed. If Amy felt the same, she didn't show it. Instead she merely smirked and shook her head. "We should get the rest of this set up. I want to take a look around the grounds when we're finished. I've never been in this part of Michigan before. I'm looking forward to seeing what this place has to offer."

"There are a lot of small waterfalls on the hiking trails," Max explained. "That was my favorite part when I was a kid."

"Then I definitely want to see them."

"I think I can make that happen."

. . .

JACK DIDN'T CARE ABOUT unpacking as much as he did kissing. The second Ivy was in the tent with him, he had his arms around her and they were rolling around on the sleeping bags he'd zipped together to make a cozy bed.

"This should be the only part of camping," he announced as they got comfortable. "Seriously, we should just live in this tent. I'm pretty sure love can fortify us."

Ivy snickered, genuinely amused. "No food?"

"You're better than food."

"And you're a smooth talker." She rolled him so he was on his back and she was straddling him. It was more of a playful position than a sexual one. "So ... what do you think of Amy?" They'd already talked about Max's girlfriend ... twice ... and yet Ivy couldn't stop fixating on the woman. "I don't think she likes me."

Jack's eyebrows flew up his forehead. "Why would you say something like that? She seems to like you just fine."

"No. I asked her to help me with the kitchen stuff and she hurried over to help Max instead."

"That doesn't mean she doesn't like you. It means she's the nervous sort." He linked his fingers with hers and grinned. "Not everyone is as bold as you, honey. Give her a few hours to settle down."

"Do you think she's afraid of me or something?"

"I think you are a handful." He lifted his head from the ground. "I happen to like a handful. Give me a kiss."

"Why? You've already kissed me ten times."

"Are you keeping score?"

"I'm ... not sure what I'm doing," Ivy admitted after a beat. "I just like torturing you."

"That's because you're a mean woman." He slid his hands up and down her hips. "Come on. I need a kiss."

"I think you just want to get frisky."

"Guilty as charged. Now ... kiss me."

Because it was something she wanted to do anyway, Ivy gladly acquiesced. She sank into the exchange as he wrapped his arms around her back and held her close. Neither one of them was sure if the kiss would lead anywhere, but the possibility of that happening flew out the window when the sound of their tent zipper going up assailed their ears.

"What the ... ?" Jack made a face as he pressed Ivy close to his chest and glared at Max, who didn't seem to be bothered by what he found inside the tent. "Are you trying to get me to kill you?"

Max ignored the pointed question. "I need your help, Ivy."

She remained where she was, her head resting on Jack's chest. "I believe I've helped you all I'm going to help you this week. I let you come camping with us because of your incessant whining even though it upset Jack. I'm done doing favors for you."

Max rolled his eyes. "Get over yourself. Am I making a fuss because you're sitting on Jack in a way that makes me want to neuter him? No. I'm resigned to the fact that you guys are going to be filthy all weekend and I don't care. I really do need your help, though."

Ivy wanted to push her brother out of the tent, but she let loose a sigh instead. "What do you want me to do?"

"Oh, don't ask him that," Jack groused. "If you start bending to his whims now he's just going to keep upping the ante. Personally, I think they should stay on their side of the campground and we'll stay on our side. I know I'm going to be outvoted on that, though."

"You definitely are," Max agreed. "We're here for romance, but I'm also trying to get to know her. She's a little closed off."

Ivy lifted her head, intrigued despite herself. "What do you mean?"

"She's just ... shy." Max plopped down on the floor of the tent, making Jack realize that he wasn't leaving anytime soon.

"Ugh." Jack kept Ivy pressed tight to him as he sat up so she wouldn't go spilling to the floor and rearranged her so she was sitting comfortably between his legs as he focused on the older Morgan sibling. "What seems to be the problem? Be specific. I have plans for your sister and I can't engage in them until you're out of this tent. Oh, and by the way, if you come back in this tent without knocking, I'm going to make you cry like a little girl."

Max rolled his eyes. "Yeah. You're a terrifying specimen of a man. My knees are quaking in fear."

"I've taken you down before," Jack reminded him.

"That's when we first met and you took me by surprise. I wasn't expecting you. Lightning doesn't strike twice and I've been watching Brazilian Jiu-Jitsu on television. I could totally take you."

Ivy's forehead wrinkled. "Is that that thing I saw you watching at the lumberyard a few weeks ago? The one where the pasty white dudes were rolling around on the floor together, right?"

"They weren't rolling around on the floor together. They were wrestling, fighting the battle of the gods."

Jack snorted as he smoothed Ivy's hair. "I believe I know exactly what sport you're talking about. Here's the thing ... your sister could take all those dudes without even breaking a sweat."

To Ivy, that sounded like an insult. "I'm strong."

"That's what I said."

"No, you said it in a mocking way." She pinched his flank. "I'm all-powerful and strong. Bow down."

Jack's smile was indulgent. "I would totally bow down if you were dressed like Wonder Woman when you delivered that line."

"Maybe when we get home." She kissed his cheek and turned back to Max, frowning when she realized he was glaring at her. "What were we talking about again?"

"How much I want to smother you both," Max replied without hesitation. "You need to focus on me." He slapped his knee for emphasis. "I'm being serious here. Amy ran down to the bathroom so she won't be gone long. I need you to listen to what I have to say ... and then advise me ... oh, and then disappear because I want to romance her without you guys trying to distract me."

"Yes, we're the ones distracting you from romance," Jack drawled.

"You are." Max was firm. "I just need help."

He looked so forlorn Ivy couldn't help taking pity on him. "You really like her, don't you?"

He nodded, sincere. "I do. I don't know how to explain it. There's something about her that calls to me. You said it was like that for you when you met my sister, Jack. I'm just trying to get her to open up. How did you get Ivy to start talking?"

"Believe it or not, your sister has never been shy when it comes to sharing things with me," Jack replied, smiling as he thought back to the beginning of his relationship with Ivy. "I can't believe it's been more than a year. In two months, we'll be married. This has been the best year of my life."

"Oh." Ivy beamed with pleasure as she leaned back and studied Jack's strong profile. "It's been the best year of my life, too."

"Oh, don't make me douse you with water," Max snapped. "I need help. Amy is loving ... and kind ... and sweet. She has the best laugh. She's just quiet and never volunteers anything. I just found out a few minutes ago that her parents are dead."

Ivy sighed, the sound long and drawn out. "Did you ask her about her parents before today?"

"No."

"Why not?"

"Because ... um ... because ... ."

Ivy already knew the answer. "Because you were too busy talking about yourself," she finished. "I love you, Max. You know that's true. You're the best big brother in the world. You have a tendency to make everything about you, though.

"As for Amy, I don't know what to tell you," she continued. "She seems to be the nervous sort. I tried talking to her myself, but I think I frighten her or something."

"You do," Max confirmed. "She thinks you're outgoing and intimidating. She likes you, but she's terrified you're going to start yelling at her the same way you did at Jack when he didn't put up the tent the way you preferred."

Ivy's expression darkened. "I didn't yell at Jack about the tent." She looked to her fiancé for confirmation. "Tell him I didn't yell at you."

"Honey, you yelled a little," Jack replied without missing a beat. "It's not a big deal, though. We tend to be loud individuals. That's simply how we communicate." He flicked his eyes to Max. "We'll try to refrain from doing that in front of Amy until she knows us better. We forget that not everyone communicates in the same manner we do."

"It's not about that," Max argued. "It's just ... I don't know how to do this. I'm not a very good relationship guy."

The expression on his face – a sad mix of worry and potential heartbreak – was enough to tug on Ivy's heartstrings. "You've got to get over yourself and focus on her," she explained, choosing her words carefully. "Instead of volunteering stories about our family and then telling another story about our family, just relate the one story and then ask her if something similar happened over the course of her life. Relationships are about give and take."

"Right." Max rubbed his forehead, his eyes cloudy. "How long was it before you guys were confiding in one another?"

"Oh, well ... ." Ivy turned to Jack, uncertain. "How long would you say it was?"

"We started talking right from the start," Jack volunteered. "We didn't talk about the big things obviously. That didn't start occurring until we started sharing dreams. We talked about our families and the other stuff fairly quickly, though."

"It was a couple of days before Jack told me about being shot," Ivy volunteered. "He only told me because of the poison ivy, though, and the fact that he had to take his shirt off so I saw his chest."

"And it was several days before your sister started confiding in me that she was afraid," Jack added. "By then I was already determined to keep her safe forever."

"See, I want to keep Amy safe forever," Max noted. "I already feel that. She opens up sometimes and then seems to catch herself. I don't know how to explain it. Something just feels off."

"Probably because you're so desperate for things to work out," Ivy volunteered. "I know how that goes. I felt that way when Jack and I first hooked up. When he took off after I was shot ... well ... it was like every doubt I ever had took me over. You're probably feeling the same way."

"I'm so glad that was brought up again," Jack muttered, earning a grin from Ivy.

"Don't worry." She patted his cheek. "I know without a shadow of a doubt you would never leave me again. You didn't even really leave me the first time. You just freaked out for twenty-four hours and then slapped yourself back together and became the best boyfriend a woman could ever hope for. I know that you're going to be a wonderful husband, too."

"Aw." Jack grinned at her and lowered his mouth to offer a sweet kiss. "I can't believe I got so lucky when I found you."

"Oh, gag me." Max rolled to his knees to crawl out of the tent. "You guys are absolutely no help. I came in here for real advice, not to watch you bounce off each other like rabbits. Good grief. You guys are sick."

Ivy squeezed Jack's hand as she called out to Max. "Just sit down and ask her questions, Max. Ask about high school ... and her favorite movies ... and what she likes to eat. All the things you like to talk about are probably the same things she likes to talk about. You just have to be patient because she does seem to be the nervous sort. She won't tell you to stop talking about yourself even though everyone would be happiest if you did."

"Ha, ha, ha." Max rolled his eyes as he slipped through the opening. "I guess your lame advice is better than no advice."

"Here's more advice," Jack called out. "If you come in here again, I'm going to beat you up. I don't care if you're going to be my brother-in-law or not."

"I will take you down with my Jiu-Jitsu." Max struck a hilarious pose. "On a different note ... thanks for listening. I'm sorry I took over your camping trip. I promise this won't become a regular thing."

"That would be a nice change of pace," Jack agreed, waiting until Max closed the zipper to ask the obvious question. "He's crazy for her, isn't he?"

Ivy nodded as she reached for the canvas flap that covered the tent window. When she yanked it down, she found Max already crossing to the trail that led down to the water spigot and bathrooms. Amy was halfway back, standing in the middle of the trail and staring at ... something. Ivy had trouble making out what had caught the woman's attention.

"What's she looking at?"

"Hmm." Jack's lips were busy on her neck and it took every ounce of strength he had to pull his attention away from the love of his life. It took him a moment to find Amy in the open expanse, and when he did, he merely shrugged. "I don't know. There's a guy over yonder putting up his own tent. I think he asked her a question ... or maybe he was hitting on her or something. Max will take care of it."

"I guess." Ivy stared a moment longer. The way Amy was looking at the man made her distinctly uncomfortable. “Maybe they know each other.”

“Maybe.” Jack moved his lips to the corner of her mouth. “Shut that thing and focus on me. I have something I want to show you.”

Despite herself, Ivy couldn’t stop herself from laughing. “That old thing? I’ve seen it a million times.”

“I’ve made some improvements.”

“Oh, really? Perhaps one more time wouldn’t hurt.”

“That’s exactly what I hoped you would say.”

Four

Ivy was a good cook ... in her own kitchen. Cooking over an open fire was another matter and it didn't help that Max kept sticking his nose in as she attempted to grill hamburgers on the new skillet Jack had purchased for the trip.

"You're making them too thick," Max complained as he studied the three patties on the metal contraption. "And what is that?" He gestured toward a third item and made a disgusted face. "Did you drop that one on the ground already? That's the one you're going to feed me, isn't it?"

Amy stood next to the picnic table mixing the pasta salad Ivy made at home and watched the banter with overt amusement.

"That's mine," Ivy snapped, her eyes lighting with annoyance. "It's a soy burger."

"Ugh." Max made a disgusted face and shifted his eyes to Jack, who was transferring beer cans into the beverage cooler. "She brought a soy burger to the woods. How can you live with her when she does stuff like that?"

Jack's fingers were chilly and wet from being in the ice and he transferred them to Ivy's hip, causing her to jump as he chuckled. "I happen to be impressed with the fact that she's a vegetarian. She's dedicated to a belief system ... and I'm proud of her for sticking to it. Don't give her grief."

Ivy slid her eyes to Jack in appreciation. "Thank you, honey."

"No, thank you, honey." He pressed a kiss to her mouth, causing Max to mime vomiting as he moved away from his sister.

"I keep thinking you guys are going to stop being so sappy, but I guess that's not happening until after the wedding, huh?"

Jack narrowed his eyes. "We're going to be sappy for the rest of our lives."

"We are," Ivy agreed, nudging Jack back in case he decided he really did want to wrestle her brother to the ground. Max's insistence upon joining their camping trip remained a major annoyance and even though she was working overtime to smooth the edges of Jack's frazzled nerves, it wasn't an easy task. "You should be glad you weren't in the truck with us for the ride up. We spent half the time talking about future children."

"Really?" Rather than being annoyed, Max looked intrigued. "How many kids are we talking about here? I picture you guys with five of them ... and they're all just as annoying as Ivy."

"If I had five more Ivys I would be a happy man," Jack shot back. "It's little Maxes we are terrified of getting."

Ivy heaved out a sigh and held out her hands. "Knock it off. I don't like that you guys are at each other's throats." In a moment of desperation, she focused on Amy. "What about you? Do you want children someday?"

Amy clearly wasn't expecting the question because her eyes went wide and half the color drained from her face. "Oh, well, I haven't given it a lot of thought. I mean ... probably one day I will. It's not a concern for right this second."

That was the most she'd said to Ivy in one speech to this point so the pink-haired peacemaker decided to run with it. "But ... you've probably thought about it a little, right?" she pressed. "Jack and I have been talking about it a lot lately. We both want kids, although we've agreed we'd like to wait a year or two."

"That's smart," Amy offered. "I mean ... you guys are just starting out. You should enjoy each other for a few years, get to know one another even better than you do now. A child changes things. Right now, you're the center of each other's worlds. If you add in a baby, then the infant will be the center of both your worlds. I think you guys will be fine when that happens but not everyone feels the same way."

Ivy found the response mildly disconcerting. "Do you speak from experience?"

"Oh, not mine." She was firm as she shook her head. "Before I moved to Shadow Lake I was friends with a girl in college. She got married before we graduated from high school and thought it was the greatest thing that ever happened to her. She accidentally got pregnant a few months later and her husband kind of melted down, said he wasn't ready for that sort of responsibility.

"He stuck around, which she thought was good at the time, but he resented her for bringing someone into the household who supplanted him from being the center of their world," she continued. "He turned into a mean guy after that. She didn't even recognize the monster he became."

Ivy opened her mouth but no sound came out. She legitimately had no idea what she was supposed to say. Thankfully, Jack picked that moment to swoop in.

"That's a big deal," he said. "She was young. That had to be frightening. Did he hurt her physically?"

"Some."

"Did she call the police? If she's still in trouble, I can offer some assistance."

"What? Oh, no, this was several years ago and they're no longer together. Besides, it was in Minnesota and not here. Everything has been handled."

"I'm glad for that." Jack moved his hand to Ivy's slim back. "How about I handle the burgers and your ... soy thing ... and you help Amy with the pasta? That way, if there are any complaints about the thickness of the burgers, your brother can take it up with me."

Ivy was thrilled with the suggestion. "I think that's a marvelous idea." She scorched Max with a dark look before moving over to the table. "I'm glad your friend managed to get away from that situation."

"I am, too." Amy's smile was small but heartfelt. "So, how many kids do you want? You must have some idea."

"Well, we've thought about it a lot." Ivy glanced over her shoulder and met Jack's steady gaze. "I think we'll be happy with two. We would prefer a boy and a girl, but I can't see us being bitterly disappointed if we have two boys or two girls."

"I don't know," Jack countered. "I want a little you to spoil. If we have two boys, I won't be disappointed, but I'm still going to want a little girl."

"You can always get another cat," Max suggested. "I've often thought Ivy has the personality of a cat. She's skittish when strangers are around and she likes to keep to herself while constantly glaring at interlopers."

Jack shot him a dirty look. "You just can't help yourself, can you?"

"Not even a little." Max offered him a haughty smirk and reached for the skillet. "I'll handle grilling duties for the evening, if you don't mind. It's not that I don't trust you but ... you've never cooked meat over an open flame."

"I grill in the backyard all the time."

"That's different."

"Jack is doing the grilling," Ivy interjected, fixing her brother with a pointed look. "Why don't you help Amy with the pasta salad, huh?"

"I think that's probably safest," Amy agreed, giggling when Max made a face behind his sister's back. "I think it's best if you let Jack handle the grilling tonight ... since he's the one who bought the food."

"See. Your girlfriend is a wise woman." Jack slid around Max and headed for the fire. "I have no idea what she's doing with you, but she's wise all the same."

"Yeah, yeah, yeah." Max made a derisive gesture as Jack strolled away. "I never get the respect I deserve. I wonder why that is."

"I think it has something to do with your attitude," Ivy replied. "Now ... help. I won't feed you if you don't help."

"You've turned mean since you started dating Jack. You used to be so nice to me. Where did the love go?"

. . .

THE FOOD WASN'T PERFECT, BUT the group was so hungry that it didn't matter. Everyone inhaled everything on their plates and then set about as a group to clean up.

"Are there bears up here?" Amy asked nervously as Jack stoked the fire and Max grabbed a bag of marshmallows. "I mean ... is that why we have to be so careful putting the food away?"

"There are bears up here," Max confirmed. "You don't need to worry about that, though. They're not aggressive. As long as we handle food properly, they won't even come around."

"If you do see one, just stay away from any babies you might see," Ivy suggested, opening one of the bags on the table and coming back with graham crackers and chocolate bars. "I think we have everything for s'mores. Where are the marshmallow roasting things?"

"They're stacked on the end of the table," Jack replied, his eyes lifting to the sky. "It got dark quick. I didn't even think about the lack of light since we're not by an illuminated highway. We should probably get those lanterns we bought and light them up."

"I'll get them," Max offered. "Where are they?"

"I think they're still in the back of the truck," Ivy replied after a moment's consideration. "I don't remember grabbing them."

"I've got the kerosene here," Jack offered. "We just forgot the lanterns."

"I'll get them." Max pressed a kiss to Amy's cheek as she slid the pasta salad into the cooler. He took a moment to whisper something to her that caused a small giggle to escape.

From across the table, Ivy watched the interaction with a mixture of trepidation and excitement. She'd often wondered what would happen to Max if he never settled down. In her head, she pictured him turning into a fifty-year-old gigolo with a plunging neckline, more gold-nugget jewelry than any one person should own, and a penchant for hitting on barely-legal girls. The fact that he seemed so enamored of Amy, a normal girl who was a few years younger but still age-appropriate, was a relief. Unfortunately, Ivy wasn't sure how she felt about Amy. The woman wasn't exactly outgoing, and Ivy couldn't help but wonder if Max would grow tired of constantly trying to draw her out of her shell and go back to his old ways.

"What are you thinking?" Jack asked, keeping his voice low as his breath tickled against her ear. "Are you wondering if we can steal all the s'mores ingredients and mess with your brother, too?"

Ivy snorted and shook her head. "No, I was just ... thinking." She flashed a smile for Amy's benefit. "Tell me about yourself," she prodded. "I know you grew up in Minnesota and graduated from a high school there, but I don't know anything else about you."

"What would you like to know?"

"I don't know. Um ... Max mentioned your parents died in a car accident."

"Yes, a few years ago."

"I'm sorry to hear that."

"I am, too," Jack added. "That must have been rough on you. I lost my father years ago, but it still hurts when I think about him. It must have been ridiculously difficult for you to lose both parents at the same time. Do you have any siblings you keep in contact with?"

"I'm an only child," Amy replied. "My parents had me late in life. They'd essentially given up having children. I enjoyed being an only child, though. They both doted on me."

Ivy felt a rush of sadness for the woman. "What about aunts and uncles? I know I would be devastated to lose my parents, but I'm especially close with my aunt Felicity. She's almost like a third parent."

"No. I don't have any aunts or uncles either. Er, I guess I have a distant aunt on my mother's side, but I don't know her. My grandparents died before I was born. It's just me."

Ivy swallowed hard. Even though there was something off about the woman – she was convinced of that – she hated to think of her feeling alone. "You have us as family now," she offered. "It's not just you any longer."

The look of profound gratitude Amy shot Ivy had her re-thinking her earlier opinion. There was every chance that Amy was simply shy, something that Ivy wasn't familiar with so she didn't understand how to grapple with the emotion.

"I think I'm going to take a bucket down to the spigot to get some water," Amy offered. "I won't be gone long, but I thought we might want it for cleaning up after eating the s'mores."

"That's probably a good idea," Ivy agreed. "You should wait for a lantern, though, just to be on the safe side."

"Oh, that's okay." Amy waved off the suggestion. "I've been down there twice. I won't be gone long. Tell Max where I went, okay?"

"Sure. No problem."

Jack continued to rub his hand over Ivy's back until he was certain Amy was out of earshot. He glanced over his shoulder to make sure Max hadn't returned and then asked the obvious question. "What do you think?"

Ivy held her hands out and shrugged. "I don't know. I feel sorry for her. I don't dislike her. She's just really closed off."

"Yeah. I think she's just nervous. Give her time to warm up. Hanging out with you and Max is daunting to some people. I know I felt a little weird the first few times we were together as a group."

"You did?" That was a surprise to Ivy. "You never showed it."

"That's because I'm macho."

She snickered. "Good to know. Do you want to help me take the s'mores ingredients to the fire and get comfortable while we're waiting for Max and Amy? If you're a good boy, we can sit on the ground and have two blankets – one for the top and one for under our bottoms – so no one will be able to see your wandering hands."

"You had me at s'mores."

"Somehow I knew that."

IVY AND JACK WERE ELBOW DEEP in s'mores when Max finally returned with the lanterns.

"They were buried under a tarp," he complained, dropping them on the ground next to the blanket Ivy and Jack shared. "They shouldn't have been that hard to find."

Ivy rolled her eyes. "Please. You were barely gone five minutes. It's not as if you worked yourself to the bone."

"Hey, it's more difficult than you might think to root around in the back of the truck without being able to see what you're touching. I kept imagining horrible things ... like spiders."

Ivy snorted. "I see you made it without being eaten by a Daddy Long Legs."

"I'm traumatized and need some attention." He furrowed his brow as he glanced around. "Where is Amy?"

"She volunteered to get water," Jack replied. "She left a few minutes ago. She shouldn't be gone long."

"You let her go by herself?" Max's eyes were accusatory when they locked with those of his future brother-in-law. "What were you thinking?"

"I was thinking that the spigot isn't far away," Jack replied blankly.

"It's dark," Max protested.

"It's only a little ways."

"Okay, let's swap out the women involved," Max snapped. "Would you have let Ivy walk down there alone?"

Ivy bristled at her brother's tone. "Don't yell at him."

"It's okay." Jack patted her hand. "He's right. I shouldn't have let her go alone." He moved to stand. "Let's go get her."

"And leave Ivy here?" Max made a comical face. "We both know that's not going to happen."

"Then we'll all go as a group," Ivy offered.

"No. I've got it." His eyes flashed with annoyance as he swiveled. "I'll find her ... and then we'll talk badly about both of you on our way back. Be prepared for the infamous Morgan stink eye when I return."

Jack snickered. "We look forward to that." He turned his attention – and lips – back to Ivy, but froze in place at the sound of a scream. He whipped his head in the direction of the main property office and narrowed his eyes. It was too dark to make out any movement, but when a second scream split the air, he hopped to his feet. "That doesn't sound good."

Max was several feet ahead of them when he broke into a run. "Amy."

Ivy read the panic that rippled off him in waves and scurried to keep up. "Wait. Max ... we'll go together."

"We'll *all* go together," Jack agreed, collecting Ivy's hand as they began to jog down the trail. "Everyone be careful you don't trip. We can't see if there are rocks or branches jutting out from the ground."

"Who cares about that?" Max was beside himself as he scanned both sides of the trail for movement. "Amy?" He screamed her name into the night. She didn't respond, though, which caused Ivy's heart to drop to her shoes.

"What do you think happened?" she asked Jack, breathless. "I mean ... she was only gone for a few minutes."

"I don't know, honey." Jack slowed his pace and stared hard into the dim light surrounding them. "No matter what, you stay right next to me. You can't see more than a few yards in any direction and we didn't bring the lanterns. Just ... don't wander."

Ivy solemnly nodded. "I'll stick close."

"Thank you." He pressed a kiss to her forehead and then increased his pace to catch up with Max. "Don't panic yet," he ordered. "We don't know that anything has happened. It could be kids playing around ... or people drinking ... or you know, other shenanigans."

"Or Amy." Max was forlorn as he caught Jack's gaze. "Where is she?"

"I ... ." Jack didn't get a chance to finish because the sound of raised voices caught his attention. He immediately pointed himself in that direction. "Both of you stay close," he instructed, his cop face firmly in place. "What happened here?"

"There's a body," one of the men replied. He had a small lantern in his hand and it only cast off enough light that his features looked somehow ghoulish. "Someone is dead."

"What?" Jack grabbed the lantern from him without asking and turned so he could see in the direction the man gestured. There, on the ground, was a woman. Her features weren't identifiable because they were covered by a mass of blond hair ... the same color hair Amy boasted.

Ivy's heart dropped to her stomach. "No way."

"Amy!" Max barreled forward, his voice ragged. "Omigod! Oh, my ... ." He let loose an anguished wail Ivy had never heard before and dropped to his knees.

Helpless, Ivy turned to Jack. "I don't understand."

That made two of them.

Five

Ivy's mouth was dry, her hands shaking, and she had no idea what to do.

Jack, however, was in his element.

"Everybody stand back," he ordered, lifting the lantern as he edged closer to the woman. He was careful not to touch anything but her neck when he pressed two fingers to her pulse point, his heart shuddering when he couldn't detect even the faintest of heartbeats. He exhaled heavily and met Max's gaze. "She's gone."

"No, no, no." Max moved to stride forward, but Ivy regained her senses fast enough to grab her brother around the waist. "Let go of me!"

"I can't," Ivy gritted out. "Let Jack do his job."

"No!" Max ripped himself from Ivy and stumbled in the direction of the body. "I can't even ... I ... this isn't happening."

Jack extended a hand to keep Max back, but the older Morgan sibling slapped it away, fury rippling through him.

"Max, you can't touch her." Jack's voice was calm, no-nonsense. "I need more light to look her over. Also, we need to call for the authorities."

"You're a cop," Max reminded him, his voice dead.

"This isn't my jurisdiction."

"You're a cop?" One of the men standing to the side, a stocky individual with brown hair and a thick mustache, appeared impressed. "I guess that's lucky for us, huh?"

"It's ... something." Jack was grim. "Ivy, can you check and see if you have a signal? If not, Max will walk you to the road to see if you can find a better one. We need to get the state police and the medical examiner in here."

Ivy nodded dumbly. "Yeah."

"I'm not walking her anywhere," Max hissed, his voice dangerously close to violent. "She can walk herself ... just like you let Amy walk herself."

Jack tugged on his limited patience. He understood Max had gone into shock or something – and he couldn't blame him – but there was no way he intended to let Ivy wander away without someone watching her back. "Max, I know you're upset—"

"You don't know anything. This is all your fault!" Max exploded with enough rage that he caused Ivy to take an inadvertent step away from her brother.

"Max, you can't blame him," Ivy squeaked out. "I'm so sorry. I'm so, so sorry. You'll never know how sorry I am. You have to let him do his job now, though. There's nothing you can do for her."

Max didn't respond. Instead, hands clenched into fists at his sides, he let out a series of exaggerated breaths that made Ivy realize he was trying to talk himself out of attacking Jack. She recognized the calming technique from when they were kids and he had to force himself from going after the individuals who bullied her on a regular basis.

Sensing he had a bit of breathing room, Jack lowered the lantern closer to the woman's features. He was trying to ascertain if there was any clear indication of violence, but he lost his train of thought when he noticed movement from the other side of the clearing.

"What's going on?" The voice asking the question was low and clearly female.

Max snapped his head in the woman's direction, his voice cracking when he finally found it. "Amy?"

"Of course it's Amy. Who else did you expect? Did something happen?"

Max didn't respond, instead swooping toward her and pulling her small body into his arms. He burst into tears as he held her, forcing her to lean around his tall frame to get a better look.

"I don't understand—" she broke off when she realized Jack was kneeling over a body. "Who is that?"

"We thought it was you." Ivy mustered a wan smile. "I'm happy it's not, for the record."

"Me, too." Max stroked his hand over the back of Amy's head. He seemed to be lost in her, something Ivy had never seen from her brother. It was fascinating. Of course, the dead body they assumed was Amy was also fascinating ... just in a different way.

"Does anyone know who she is?" Jack asked, extending his finger toward Ivy. "Place that call, honey. We need help out here."

Ivy finally remembered Jack had given her a task to complete and wordlessly nodded. She checked her cell phone for bars and was relieved to find she had three.

"I think she might've been staying at the camp over there," the mustached man gestured vaguely into the darkness behind him. "If it's the woman I'm thinking of, she was with her husband ... or maybe a boyfriend. It was just the two of them. No kids."

"That's helpful." Jack smiled in gratitude at the man. "Ivy, make the call."

She was already doing it. Even though she felt relief at the fact that Amy was well and whole, that didn't change the fact that there was a dead woman at the campground.

"So much for a quiet weekend," she muttered as she lifted the phone to her ear. "This wasn't what we expected."

"No," Jack agreed. "It is what it is, though. We have to do what we can for her."

Ivy wholeheartedly agreed.

THE STATE POLICE BROUGHT PORTABLE lighting and multiple investigators with them when they landed. Within the blink of an eye, the area surrounding the registration office was illuminated. Ivy found that the light managed to take the edge off her fear.

"Maybe you should take Amy back to the campsite," she suggested as the lead investigator, Trooper John Winters, pulled Jack aside to get a full report.

"Not yet," Winters ordered, extending a finger in their direction. "We need to question everyone before we allow anyone to leave."

"Okay. Sorry." Ivy sent Jack an apologetic glance and then moved closer to her brother and his girlfriend. "Did you see anything, Amy?"

The woman was white as a sheet. If Ivy didn't know better, she would believe she was only on her feet because Max was holding her up. As for her brother, he seemed to be stronger now, closer to his normal self. He didn't look happy, though.

"Of course she didn't see anything," Max snapped. "She would've said something if she saw it going down. What are you thinking?"

Ivy held up her hands in surrender. "I'm sorry. I'm just trying to get the time to pass faster."

"It's okay," Amy said quickly, shaking her head at Max before focusing on Ivy. "I didn't mean for this to happen. I was just looking around by the trees over there. They have raspberries I noticed earlier and I was tasting a few." She looked sheepish. "I was over there longer than I intended and then I realized I was hearing voices and I thought I recognized Max's voice but couldn't be sure."

It was a weird time to be picking raspberries, but Ivy kept that comment to herself. "Did you see that woman earlier?"

"I don't know." Amy shrugged, seemingly helpless. "I think I saw a blond woman about four campsites away from where we're staying. The first time I went down for water I saw her with a man. I only remember because they seemed to be arguing over putting up the tent. I just assumed they were like you and Jack, though."

Ivy wasn't thrilled with the comparison. "Well ... she's dead now."

"Which isn't Amy's fault," Max hissed.

"You need to calm down," Ivy shot back, the first hints of anger taking hold. "I'm not trying to be mean but ... come on. I never said any of this was Amy's fault. Why are you jumping all over me?"

"Because you let her walk down here alone," Max replied without hesitation. "That could've been her. I thought it was her." His voice cracked again, telling Ivy he was back to being morose.

"Max, I understand this has been an ordeal for you." Ivy kept her voice low so Winters wouldn't overhear her. "I'm sorry you're upset. I mean it. I'm truly sorry. You can't act like this, though. It's not my fault."

"It's Jack's fault. He should've walked her down to the spigot."

"We both should've walked her down here. If you want to be mad, aim it at me. We didn't think about it and that's on us. She's safe, though. You need to pull it together."

The look Max shot her was withering. "Maybe you need to pull it together," he countered. "Maybe you're the one who is acting like a jerk. Have you ever considered that?"

Rather than respond, Ivy waved a hand in his direction and turned back to Jack. She was done dealing with her brother and his horrible mass of moods this evening. It was good timing because Winters was cutting across to talk to her.

"Detective Harker explained what happened," he started. "I just need corroboration from you."

Ivy was familiar with how police investigators worked so she ran through the story from the beginning, leaving nothing out. When she was finished, Winters moved on to Max and Amy to question them. Since Amy was separated from the small group, Winters' questions for her were different.

"Did you hear any noises when you entered the area?" he asked.

"No. I wasn't really listening for anything, though. I mean ... I was in my own little world. We had a wonderful dinner and I was getting water. I just planned on having a few berries because they looked so good earlier and then heading back. Although ... I put down that huge jug thing over there somewhere when I heard Max's voice. I'm afraid I still don't have the water."

"That's okay," Jack offered quickly. "I'll find it and bring it back. You don't have to worry about it."

"You definitely don't have to worry about it," Max echoed darkly.

Ivy pressed her lips together to keep from exploding at her brother. She figured that was the last thing the trooper needed to bear witness to. She wasn't sure how long she could contain her annoyance, though.

"Do any of you remember seeing this woman earlier in the evening?" Winters asked. "I'm talking about when it was still light out."

"I didn't," Ivy replied. "I stuck close to camp, though."

"I think I might have seen her," Amy offered. "She was over in that direction with a man. I don't know if he was her husband or boyfriend."

"Did you witness them saying anything to one another?"

"Oh, well ... ." Amy looked decidedly uncomfortable as she shifted from one foot to the other.

"It's okay, Amy," Jack prodded. "Just tell Trooper Winters what you saw and that will be the end of it."

Amy nodded and heaved out a sigh. "They looked to be fighting," she said finally. "Not like really fighting or anything. I mean ... there was no physical violence and they weren't screaming at one another. As far as I could tell, they were arguing about how best to erect the tent."

"Which is the same argument Ivy and I had when we arrived," Jack volunteered. "It doesn't necessarily mean anything."

"It doesn't," Winters agreed. "I can't ignore it either."

JACK SENT IVY BACK TO CAMP with Max and Amy. He opted to stay behind and help as long as he could. He promised Ivy he wouldn't be long, fixed Max with a heavy stare that warned retribution if he put up a fuss, and then sent them on their way.

Max groused about Jack's attitude the entire way back.

"He acts like he's smarter than everybody else ... and stronger than everybody else ... and the boss of everyone."

Ivy, who had managed to keep her mouth shut for longer than she envisioned, finally lost it. "I'm sick of your crap," she hissed, poking her brother in the chest ... hard. "I'm so sick of it you have no idea. You can't blame Jack for this. He didn't do anything and he doesn't deserve your ire."

"He let Amy walk to the spigot by herself," Max shot back. "That could have been her and not that poor woman."

"You don't know that." Ivy wasn't in the mood for Max's attitude. "We don't know why she was killed. We don't even know if she was killed. She could've tripped and hit her head for all we know. It's not as if there was blood or a knife sticking out of her."

Max slid his arm around Amy's shoulders as she shuddered. "And thank you for that visual right before we go to bed. I can see Jack has been a tremendous influence on you."

Ivy continued stomping when they hit the campground. They'd left the fire roaring and she knew she had to douse it before sleep. "I can't even look at you right now," she muttered. "Go to bed. Maybe you'll resemble the brother I grew up with in the morning."

"I am the brother you grew up with," he spat. "I'm the same brother that stood up for you when the bullies were picking on you ... and stayed home from dances simply because you didn't have a date. That's why I'm so angry. I never would've let you walk down there alone. The fact that you let Amy is just ... I can't even find the right words."

"You don't need to find the right words," Amy interjected, giving him a small shove toward their tent. "I'm fine. I'm right here. I think you should lay down and get some rest. I'll join you in a few minutes."

"No. I want you to stay with me." Max grabbed her hand. "We've been separated enough for one night."

"It will just be a few minutes." Amy didn't back down, instead giving Max another shove. "I will be right behind you. I promise."

He was reticent but did as she asked, his eyes briefly locking with those of his sister. There was a warning there that wasn't missed by Ivy. She didn't acknowledge it, though. Instead she merely exhaled and rubbed her forehead as Amy fixed her with a sympathetic look.

"I've never seen him this way before," she started, apology lacing her words.

"Don't worry about it." Ivy found she was glad to have the woman on her side. "He's just ... worked up. We really did think that was you. He fell apart."

"I can see that. It's not okay for him to take out his anger on you, though. If I felt I needed someone to walk to the spigot with me, I would've asked."

"Yeah, but we shouldn't have let you go. Our lives are weird enough that we knew better. I'm sorry I didn't volunteer to go with you."

"It wouldn't have changed anything. Literally. I wasn't hurt. I don't plan on being hurt. I'm fine."

"I'm really glad you are." Ivy reached over and clasped the woman's hand. "I know I don't know you well, but my brother really likes you. I mean ... *really* likes you. Please forgive him for acting like a fool this evening."

"There's nothing to forgive. I understand that he's upset. I would be upset in his shoes. I'm going to see he gets some sleep and hopefully he'll be back to his normal self in the morning."

"That would be nice." Ivy released her hand. "Sweet dreams."

"You, too. Although ... are you okay sleeping alone? You're more than welcome to come inside with us if you're afraid to sleep alone."

"No, she's not," Max called from inside the tent.

For the first time in hours, Ivy found herself laughing. "I'll be fine. Jack won't be long. Someone would have to be crazy to stick around with all these cops on site."

"Good point. Goodnight."

"Goodnight to you, too."

IVY WAS CONVINCED SHE WOULDN'T be able to sleep, but she slipped under within a few minutes of crawling between the sleeping bags. She was out cold when Jack finally joined her well after midnight. He stripped down to his boxer shorts and slid in beside her, wrapping his arms around her waist as she murmured and shifted.

"I'm sorry I woke you," he whispered, kissing her on the forehead when she wrapped herself around him, resting her head on his chest. "I didn't mean to be so long."

"It's okay," she said, struggling to make her brain catch up. "Do you know anything?"

"Very little. Her name is Stacy Shepherd. She's twenty-five, was here with her husband, and her neck was snapped."

Ivy's eyes flew open. "Was it an accident?"

He shrugged. "We don't know yet. The medical examiner seems to think that's unlikely but there's always the chance that she tripped headfirst going down that little hill. He won't know more until he has a chance to really get in there and look at things."

Ivy wrinkled her nose. "That's … lovely."

"I'm sorry." He gave her a soft kiss. "The husband showed up not long after you left. His name is Gordon Shepherd. He said he was out night fishing in the creek and had no idea anything happened. Trooper Winters opted to take him in for questioning. I don't know if his story will stand up."

"It sounds a little weak, huh?"

"It does, but no one saw them together in the two hours leading up to her death. Everyone who saw her right before and after dinner said she was up there alone. He could've gone night fishing. It's an actual thing."

"Yeah." Ivy kissed his strong jaw and wrapped her arms tightly around him. "Max is still angry. He didn't stop complaining the entire way back to the campground. Amy promised to talk to him but … I don't know. I don't like that he blames us."

"I'm not exactly happy about that either. That being said, if you'd walked down there alone and he hadn't gone with you, I would be put out. He has a right to his anger."

"Even though he's only here because he pushed his way into our vacation?"

"I'm trying to be the bigger man."

Ivy laughed despite herself. "You're definitely the bigger man."

"Thank you." He gave her another kiss and snuggled her close. "Now I think we should go to sleep. We'll know more about what happened tomorrow. I mean … it's still possible that it was an accident."

Ivy could tell by his tone that he didn't believe that. "Yeah. Sleep sounds good." She brushed her lips against his. "I love you, Jack. I'm not angry with you for anything that happened … and I'm sorry that this vacation is already going like the last one."

"Don't remind me. I'm starting to think we're not meant to camp."

"Don't give up just yet. Tomorrow is another day."

"And I'm looking forward to it."

Six

The sun shining through the tent window Ivy forgot to close the night before woke her and Jack several hours later. Jack made a groaning sound as he shifted and brought his arm up to cover his eyes.

"Can someone turn off the light?" he groused.

Ivy chuckled as she rolled to her knees and grabbed the hanging piece of canvas. She slipped it back into place, which immediately made the tent ten shades darker, and flopped back onto the sleeping bag with Jack. "Better?"

"I have you. My life is perfect." He slipped his arm around her back and nestled her close. "Did you sleep okay? I was down for the count so fast I didn't even check to make sure you were out before shutting down."

Ivy furrowed her brow. "Do you always wait for me to fall asleep first?"

"Not always. Just when I think there's a chance you might be upset."

"I'm not upset."

Jack cocked an eyebrow and forced open an eye. "You're not upset, huh?" He didn't believe that for a second. He knew her too well. "So, that means you're going to throw your arms around your brother and give him a long hug when you see him this morning, right?"

Ivy wrinkled her nose. "I don't know if I would go that far," she hedged. "It's not because I'm upset, though. I'm simply not much of a hugger."

He snorted, genuinely amused. "Yes, you withhold affection with the best of them." He poked her side and grinned. "Do you know why I fell in love with you?"

"Because I'm sugar and spice and everything nice."

"I know you meant that as a joke, but in a way, it's true. You are one of the sweetest women I've ever met. You're also feisty. Your heart is bigger than a skyscraper, too."

"Oh, geez. You're laying it on a bit thick."

He chuckled. "I fell in love with you because you have a giving heart and you love freely. I saw the way you were with Max — the way you joked and adored him without giving it a thought — and I knew I wanted to be loved by you, too."

Ivy stared hard into his eyes. "Please." She let loose an inelegant snort. "You fell in love with me because I cooked for you and we started sharing dreams. We were connected from the start. This little manipulative thing you're trying here to get me to make up with Max isn't going to work. I know darned well my relationship with him didn't have a thing to do with why we bonded."

Jack was philosophical. "I had to try."

"Well, it's not going to work. I'm still mad at Max. I can't help it. The way he treated us last night ... it was unfair. We didn't earn his wrath."

"Ivy, when someone you care about is in danger, sometimes human reactions don't follow a set plan," he hedged. "Max thought Amy died. That had to shake him. Heck, it shook me and I barely know her."

Ivy thought back to the way her heart pounded and her stomach threatened to revolt. "Yeah. I didn't know what to make of it. I felt as if I was mired in quicksand and there was no way out. It was like I was trapped in an echo chamber and I didn't know how to comfort my own brother."

"Your brother is not a perfect man. He's still your best friend. He was upset last night. He was manic. How do you think I would've responded under the same circumstances? If I thought you were dead on the ground and then you turned up, you couldn't pry me off you with a crowbar. I would be angry at the people who let you walk alone in the dark and created the situation, too."

Ivy immediately balked. "We didn't create the situation. I'll agree that we probably shouldn't have left her alone to walk to the main building by herself. That wasn't smart. She's okay, though, and Max is treating us like criminals. It's stupid ... and I don't like it."

"I'm sure he doesn't like it either."

"Why are you taking his side?"

"Because I know how crushed I would've been if that had been you and I'm open to giving him the benefit of the doubt. I happen to think he's going to be better this morning — maybe not apologetic, but definitely better. You can't hold this against him. Do you have any idea how awful I would be under the same circumstances?"

Ivy could've lied. She thought about it, although only briefly. She knew exactly how Jack would've reacted because she would've responded in the same way. She would've been a mess. The fact that Jack had a point about letting Max off the hook bothered her, though. "I'm not playing nice until he apologizes." Her tone was firm. "I mean it."

"Well, then it should be a stressful and uncomfortable day." He kissed her forehead. "I, for one, am looking forward to it."

Ivy ignored him and snuggled closer. "Five more minutes and then we can go out and greet the day. I'm as eager as you to hear more about Stacy Shepherd."

Jack doubted that was true, but he let the comment pass. Ivy was as keyed up as Max. She just didn't realize it.

It was going to be a long day.

IVY AND JACK WERE ALREADY sitting in front of a fresh fire drinking coffee and tea when Max let himself out of the tent he shared with Amy. She was still inside waking herself up — she was a slow starter in the mornings — and she insisted Max greet his sister and future brother-in-law sans her watchful stare. Max had a feeling that was because she wanted them to get any residual arguments out of their systems before she joined them.

Honestly, he didn't blame her. He wasn't exactly proud of his reaction the previous evening.

"Hey," he muttered as he shuffled closer to the fire. "Is that coffee?"

Ivy hiked an eyebrow as she slid him a sidelong look. "I don't know. Do you think it's coffee?"

"Oh, geez." Jack pinched the bridge of his nose and stared at the sky. "If you guys are going to start fighting, tell me now because I need to add bourbon to my coffee. I can't take a morning of snarking."

"You live with Ivy," Max pointed out. "She snarks at you over breakfast every single day."

"Yes, but she's cute when she does it," Jack shot back. "I don't happen to find you as cute as I find her."

"That's probably a relief." Max, uncomfortable, shifted from one foot to the other. "So ... um ... about last night."

Ivy's expression never changed as she focused on her tea. She wasn't a coffee drinker so she brought tea bags to fuel her caffeine habit. "If you start yelling at us, I'm going to wrestle you down and fill your mouth with dirt," she muttered.

Jack shot her a quelling look. "Don't pick a fight with your brother. He's trying to apologize."

"I'm not trying to apologize," Max argued hurriedly. "It's just ... I might have been a little loud and obnoxious last night. I stress *might*."

Jack maintained his cool. "And that's not an apology?"

"No." Max was firm as he shook his head. "I'm not sorry for what I said. Not even a little. I happen to believe that you were in the wrong for letting her leave the campsite without an escort."

Jack sighed. "I actually agree with that. If you'd done the same to Ivy, I would've melted down and been a lot worse than you were last night. I acknowledge that and apologize. I shouldn't have let Amy go alone. I honestly wasn't thinking."

"You couldn't have known what would happen," Max offered. "It's just ... I've never felt that way before." His expression was earnest enough that it melted some of the icy resolve surrounding Ivy's heart.

"I never felt fear like that before. I guess that's probably how you felt when Ivy was shot, huh?"

Jack's smile dipped. "I wish people would stop bringing that up. It gives me nightmares."

Ivy absently patted his arm. "We'll stop talking about it."

"I didn't agree to that." Max held a straight face for an extended beat and then his lips curved. "I didn't mean to take out my frustrations on you guys last night. I realize now that wasn't fair. It's just ... I was afraid."

Ivy took pity on him exactly the way Jack knew she would. "It's okay to be afraid, Max." Her voice was soft. "I've been afraid numerous times in my life. You can't turn on the people who are on your side, though. That's not fair ... or smart. And, for the record, I'll always be on your side because that's who I am."

"I know." Max was relieved as he stepped forward and pressed a light kiss to the top of his sister's head. The tension that had been dragging at both of them since they woke drifted away. "I'm sorry about everything. I just ... I fell apart. I'll try not to let it happen again, but I can't guarantee I'm capable of doing that."

"Don't worry about it." Jack waved off the apology. "I've melted down a time or two when it comes to your sister. It happens. I don't think we need to dwell on it."

Max's grin widened. "Great. I'm glad we're all in love with each other again."

"I wouldn't go that far," Jack countered.

Max ignored him. "So, I was thinking we would have some breakfast and then take a hike past the waterfalls. Amy has never seen waterfalls and she seems a bit antsy this morning. I think what happened last night affected her more than she's willing to admit. I already told her it was a plan so ... let's get to breakfast, huh?"

His expression was so hopeful that Jack couldn't slap him back, even though he really wanted to. Instead, he waited until Max returned to the tent to speak. "I'm never going to get you alone this trip, am I?"

"What are you talking about? You romanced my socks off yesterday and we spent five minutes snuggling alone in bed this morning." Ivy snickered as he pinned her with a dirty look. "Oh, wait. Are you insinuating you wanted to romance me on a private hike?"

"No, I'm flat out saying it. You made these waterfalls sound as if they were magical. I wanted them to be magical for both of us."

"And you don't think they will be if we bring Max and Amy along for the ride?"

"I don't think they're going to be anywhere near as magical as I initially anticipated. Let's just leave it at that."

"It's important to him." She kept her voice low. "He apologized. I can tell he's still a little nervous. As for Amy, she might actually be traumatized from what happened last night. She got lucky that she didn't run into Stacy on that hill ... or get mistaken for her ... or accidentally stumble across a kill in progress. She might be a little shaky and prefer a bigger group."

Jack narrowed his eyes. "You're just making excuses because Max was right about everybody being in love again ... mostly you and your brother."

"You make it sound gross." Ivy leaned forward and pressed a kiss to the corner of his mouth. "Don't make my relationship with my brother sound gross. I don't like that."

"Fair enough. I want time alone just the two of us this afternoon to make up for the morning hike, though. I insist."

"I believe I can make that happen."

"You'd better or I'm going to beat the crap out of your brother."

"Duly noted."

EVEN THOUGH HE WAS INITIALLY reticent, Jack found he enjoyed the hike. The park's main draw wasn't one big set of falls. It was hundreds of small sets, and he found that he enjoyed watching the waterfall more than he initially envisioned.

"It's really gorgeous here," he noted, shifting. He expected to find Ivy standing next to him but instead he found Max. "You guys must've really enjoyed visiting this place when you were kids, huh?"

Max enthusiastically nodded. "We really. We found it by a fluke, too."

"How's that?"

"Mom was supposed to book a specific campground that's farther north when we were kids. She was late even though Dad warned her it would fill up quickly. She found this place on the map and booked without telling him until we were basically on top of the campground and then she pointed and said 'oh, that's where we're staying.' My dad was confused but pulled in. Then she told him the whole story. He was completely irritated but ended up falling in love with this place. After that we came every year."

"I can see why." Jack bent over and picked up a stone so he could skip it against the slow-moving water. "I'm glad you made up with your sister. She was more upset about what happened than she wanted to let on."

Max turned sheepish. "I shouldn't have yelled at her the way I did. It's just ... it's like I lost control of my head. I couldn't make sense of anything that was happening."

"I get that," Jack acknowledged. "I've felt that way about Ivy a time or two. That's why I didn't take it personally. Still, she's your sister. She would never purposely hurt you."

"Do you think I don't know that? I was just overwrought. I don't know any other way to explain it. I didn't mean to hurt her feelings. I'll apologize again if you think it will make her feel better."

"You don't need to do that. She's fine. She's over having a good time with Amy." He inclined his chin toward the two women, who had taken off their shoes and were splashing in the shallow water as they conversed. "Just keep it in mind for the future. As for what happened, I was in the wrong. I'm sorry."

"It's over." Max made a dismissive hand gesture. "Amy is here and whole. She's still shy — and I'm working on drawing her out — but she's here. That's the most important thing."

Jack fixed his eyes on the two women and smirked. "It might be good that she's spending time with Ivy. If anyone can beat the shyness out of her, it's your sister."

Max made a horrified face. "I don't want her to be like Ivy."

"You would be so lucky."

"And you're blinded by love."

"There are worse things to be blinded by."

"MAX SEEMS BETTER TODAY," Ivy noted as she walked in the shallow water close to the shoreline. There was nothing she liked better than wading in the tepid water. "I'm glad he calmed down some."

"Me, too." Amy looked legitimately relieved as she crossed in front of Ivy. "I thought he was going to be ranting and raving for hours last night, but he fell asleep the second he climbed into the sleeping bags. Then, when he woke up this morning, he was perfectly fine."

"Max is one of those guys who angers quickly but gets over it quickly, too. He's a good guy."

"He's definitely a good guy." Amy was earnest as she fixed Ivy with an odd stare. "I care about him a great deal."

Ivy smirked. "I figured."

"No, I really mean it. I've seen you watching me a bit, as if you can't figure out what he sees in me. I can't figure it out either. I want you to know that I have legitimate feelings for him. He's important to me."

Ivy was ashamed that she'd made Amy feel out of place. "It's not that I can't figure out what he sees in you," she said hurriedly. "It's just ... I've never seen my brother this way with a woman before." She opted for the truth. "He's a good guy, but he hasn't always had the best taste in women. I just wanted to make sure you weren't like some of the others ... which you're not."

Amy laughed, the sound warming up the morning air. "It's okay. I figure it will take us a bit to get to know one another and then we'll like each other, too. I just don't want you to dismiss me out of hand before it's necessary."

"I would never do that." Ivy was sincere as she smiled. "Trust me. I ... ." She trailed off when a man appeared out of the trees. He looked ragged, as if he'd been wandering around for days, and he weaved back and forth as he wandered toward the trail. "I wonder who that is."

Amy glanced over her shoulder and frowned. "That's the man with the dead girl."

"What?" Ivy's eyes widened. "Are you sure?"

Amy immediately bobbed her head. "I'm definitely sure. Do you know if the police found him yesterday for questioning?"

Ivy searched her memory of the things Jack told her when he returned to the tent. She'd been sleepy but made a legitimate attempt to listen. "I'm pretty sure they already questioned him. He said he was night fishing, which I don't necessarily believe. I still think we should tell Jack." She swiveled and searched for her fiancé, breathing out a sigh of relief when she caught sight of him about fifty feet down. He was with Max and they seemed to be having a good time tossing rocks into the water while laughing uproariously.

"Jack." She called out his name with what she hoped was calm abandon. She didn't want to give the man a reason to panic or run.

Jack slid his eyes to her, smiled, and then noticed that she was not-so-subtly jerking her finger toward the shore. He slid his eyes in that direction and frowned when he saw what had gotten her attention. The husband of the victim was out and about — which he found surprising since he was under the impression that the police had no intention of releasing him — and he was wandering aimlessly, as if drunk, between the tree line and the water.

"Who is that?" Max asked, confused.

"The prime suspect in the death last night," Jack replied grimly, dropping the rocks he carried. "Come on. Let's check on the girls and make sure he's not off his rocker or anything."

Seven

His name was Gordon Shepherd and he'd been married to the victim for three years. Jack was the first to approach him. He'd seen the man the previous evening, but they'd never been properly introduced.

"Sir, are you turned around?"

Gordon cocked his head to the side at the intrusion, his lips perpetually curved down. "I don't know where I am."

"I can see that." Jack moved in front of Max and sent Ivy a stern look. She knew exactly what message he was sending without saying a word. *Move and I'll strangle you myself.*

Since she was nervous, Ivy was fine staying in the water. It served as a barrier of sorts between her and the man and she was thankful for it. "What's the last thing you remember?"

Jack was a tall man and Gordon had to tip his head up to look at him when they were face to face.

"I remember ... I don't know. It's all a blur. I keep hoping I'm going to wake up and this will be nothing more than a bad dream."

Even though Jack was suspicious of the man, stirrings of pity wafted through him. "Your wife was the one found last evening, correct?"

Gordon nodded, his lower lip trembling as he gasped out a breath. "They say she's dead, but I don't believe them. I think they're wrong and she's out here somewhere. They wouldn't let me see her, not at all. They said they had to talk to me and they wouldn't let me see her. She wasn't there when I got back."

"That's probably for the best," Jack said gently, exchanging a quick look with Max, who had positioned himself between the women in the water and the confused man. "Did they let you go?"

"Let me go?" Gordon repeated the words as if they were alien to him and he wasn't grasping the meaning. "I don't ... were they supposed to keep me?"

"I don't think he's slept," Max offered in a low voice. "He seems dazed."

"He also smells like a brewery," Jack supplied. "I think I can guess how he spent his evening."

"Would you do any different?" Max was earnest. "If it was Ivy ... ?" He trailed off.

Since the notion was enough to make Jack want to curl into a ball and shut out the world, he kept his focus on Gordon. "What time did the state police cut you loose?"

"It was in the middle of the night." Bitterness tinged Gordon's words. "They asked me a bunch of questions, treated me like a criminal. They said that they wanted to make sure that something bad didn't happen."

"Did you hurt your wife?" Jack's question was blunt, but he didn't care. As a man who loved a woman with every fiber of his being, he couldn't imagine ever hurting her. If this man killed his wife, he didn't deserve pity. He deserved something much, much worse. "Did you kill her?"

"You sound like the cops." Gordon's gaze was accusatory. "I would never hurt my wife. I loved her. I mean ... things weren't always perfect between us. She was bossy like you wouldn't believe. You have no idea how bossy she was. I loved her, though. I didn't kill her. Why would I do that?"

A small smile played at the corners of Jack's mouth as he flicked his gaze to Ivy. She was watching the show with overt interest. There was no fear in her expression. She trusted him implicitly.

"I know a little something about dating a bossy woman," Jack offered after a beat. "That's nothing to kill over, I would agree. The thing is, your story leaves a little to be desired. You were fishing at night? Why would you leave your wife alone like that?"

Gordon made a protesting sound with his mouth. "We camp all the time. We go every other weekend in the summer. That's the entire summer. She has her things she likes to do — like sit around the fire and read a book while eating popcorn — and I have my things I like to do. That includes fishing. We've always done things this way. I thought she was safe at the campsite. Why wouldn't she be? There were people all around."

He had a point, Jack internally mused. Stacy should've been safe at the campsite. That was one of the reasons he didn't think twice about Amy walking to the community spigot by herself. "Did the police tell you how she died?"

"No. They just said they were investigating and they would get back to me. Can you believe that? They'll get back to me. They said I can't leave the campsite. I don't want to be here any longer, though. I want to go home. I want ... my mom."

The man's reaction almost broke Jack's heart. Of course, it could be remorse, too, he reminded himself. It was possible Gordon flew off the handle in a moment of rage and legitimately regretted it.

"I think you should go back to your campsite," he said gently. "You need to rest ... and maybe lay off the beer. I'm sure the troopers will be back around this afternoon and they might have questions if you're not there."

Gordon made a face. "I didn't hurt my wife."

"I'm not saying you did. You haven't slept, though. That much is obvious. You need to lie down and get a grip on yourself. Your wife needs you now."

"My wife is dead. She doesn't need anything."

"Fair enough. Would she be a fan of the way you're handling this, though? Is this the legacy you want to leave her?"

"No." The man sank to the ground and buried his head in his hands. "She would be angry … and boss me around. She would tell me to suck it up. I wish she was here to boss me around again."

Jack understood the feeling. "I wish she was, too. She's not, though. I'm truly sorry. You really should head back."

"Yeah, I'll head back. I'll sleep. Then, when I wake up, all of this will have been a nightmare. I'll tell her about it and she'll order me not to dream about anything like that again. That's a good idea."

Jack knew better. The man wasn't dreaming. When he woke, he would feel the loss even more keenly. Whether it was regret or remorse fueling him, he had no doubt about that.

THE STATE POLICE WERE HOLDING COURT in front of the administrative building when they returned to the campgrounds. The way Trooper Winters raised his hand told Jack that they'd been waiting for him. He found that interesting.

"Come on." He linked his fingers with Ivy's and tugged her in that direction.

"I doubt they want me," she argued. "I thought I could go back to camp and take a nap. I didn't sleep very well last night."

Max cast her a sheepish look. "Sorry about that."

"You're only partly to blame," she replied. "I couldn't get that woman out of my head. No one is to blame for that."

"We don't know that yet," Jack cautioned. "You can take a nap in a few minutes, though. I might join you. For now, I would prefer it if you stuck close to me."

Ivy thought about arguing but didn't see the point. She figured the trooper wanted to discuss things with Jack on a superficial level, which meant the conversation wouldn't take long.

"We're going to head back to camp," Max volunteered. "I think a nap sounds divine."

Ivy rolled her eyes but waved them off. There really was no need for everyone to visit with the trooper.

Winters appeared eager when he caught sight of Jack. "I went up to your campsite, but you guys were gone. I wasn't sure if you would be back."

"We wouldn't leave all our stuff," Jack explained. "Most of it is new because I'm something of a camping novice."

"You mentioned that last night." Winters's eyes were kind when they locked with Ivy's somber orbs. "I hear you're the professional camper. My brother Nick and I used to camp a lot when we were kids. We never came to this place, though. I'm not even that familiar with the area, but my fiancée is pregnant and due to give birth in about two months. There was an opening here that needed to be filled and my boss agreed to double the time I get off after the birth if I fill in for two weeks ... so here I am."

"It must be hard to be away from your fiancée," Ivy noted. "Is she okay with you being gone?"

"My brother and sister-in-law are there. We're all tight. They're watching her and we Skype every night so she can yell at me. It's like being home."

Ivy's lips swished. She found the trooper funny and didn't blame him for taking the offer to work in the Upper Peninsula. In truth, he was doing the best thing for his new family even though it was a trial right now. "Your fiancée sounds like a woman I would like."

"I bet you would." Winters flashed one more smile and then focused on Jack. "I just got the preliminary autopsy report. Another more in-depth report will be issued in a few hours. The medical examiner wants to be sure, but he believes that the radial crack on Mrs. Shepherd's neck seems to indicate that there's no way she could've sustained the injury by a fall. They want to be sure, though, so he's getting a second opinion."

"That makes sense." Jack stroked his chin with one hand and moved the other to Ivy's slim back. He wanted her close. Death always made him overprotective. She was almost used to that now, although she still put up a fight. "We just saw Gordon Shepherd by the falls."

Winters's eyes sparked with interest. "Really? He's out sightseeing?"

"He's most definitely not out sightseeing. He's ... in a weird place. I don't want to judge him too harshly because it seems unfair, but he smelled as if he'd been drinking for hours straight. His eyes were red and bleary. He'd obviously been crying. He keeps referring to it as a dream he's going to wake up from."

"I think we all wish that. This is the first homicide I've covered since landing. They're simply not frequent in this area."

"That's not a bad thing," Jack argued. "I used to be a detective in Detroit. I grew numb to the violence there but much prefer the simpler life in Shadow Lake. My mother thought I would grow bored quickly, but that hasn't happened."

Winters smirked. "I think that probably has something to do with your friend." His eyes landed on Ivy's engagement ring. "I guess I'm not the only one looking down the barrel of the marriage gun."

Ivy scowled. "If you think of it as a punishment, why are you getting married in the first place?"

"Because I love her." Winters's answer was simple, and enough to placate Ivy, although only marginally. "We're both bossy people and we like to bust each other's chops. I have a feeling our kid is going to be the mouthiest redhead to ever hit the Midwest. I'm fine with it, though. I hope she looks exactly like her mother."

"It's a girl?" Ivy was intrigued despite herself.

"We don't know. Christy wants to be surprised. She also wants to wait until she loses the baby weight to get married. I would already be calling her 'my wife' if I had my druthers. She gets her way on this one, though."

Ivy liked the matter-of-fact way the man spoke. It was clear he loved his fiancée. He was just a blowhard. Since she was related to Max, she understood exactly how that worked. "I think you'll be a good father."

"Yes, well, I'm nervous. I think I will be, too, though." He winked at Ivy and then locked gazes with Jack. "We don't have enough to hold the husband yet. I plan on hanging around the campgrounds until word comes in from the medical examiner, though. Once it's ruled a homicide, we're going to arrest him."

"On what evidence?" Jack queried. "He claims he was fishing."

"We have a gentleman who was down at the exact spot where Mr.

Shepherd claims he was fishing. He says he was the only one there. That's enough for me. We need to get him into custody before he decides to run."

Jack's stomach gave a small heave. "I was kind of hoping he was innocent. I felt sorry for him when we saw him. I guess I shouldn't have let him get to me, but he appeared legitimately lost."

Ivy slid closer to Jack, lending him a bit of her warmth. "I did, too. I found myself believing him. I guess it's possible he feels really sorry for what he did and that's what we're noticing but ... I guess you know best."

"I don't feel as if I know anything," Winters countered. "That's what the prosecutor wants, though. It's sort of out of my hands."

"Well, here's hoping the second opinion comes back and it's ruled an accident. I don't know how I would deal with anything like that but ... well ... it's better than murder." His expression was rueful when he turned to Ivy. "This was supposed to be a quiet camping trip. It's starting to look like those don't exist in our world, huh?"

Ivy patted his shoulder. "Don't worry, big guy. I'll protect you. And, hey, don't give up on camping yet. You'll be going with me and any future kids we have whether you like it or not."

Yes, Jack knew what it was like to deal with a bossy woman. He wouldn't have it any other way, though. "I'm sure we'll be able to work something out."

BY THE TIME JACK AND Ivy reached the campsite, all they wanted was a nap ... and private time. Even though Jack enjoyed his future brother-in-law's company, he remained miffed that his plans had gone up in smoke the moment Max invited himself along on their camping trip.

Unfortunately, his sexy nap plans looked to be going out the window, too, because Max and Amy were not only up but talking to another man in the middle of the campground when they arrived.

"Is something wrong?" Jack was instantly alert.

"No." Max's smile was easy and engaging. "Our neighbor stopped by for a visit and to invite us fishing. We got to talking and lost track of time. What did the trooper say?"

"They're in a holding pattern waiting for a final determination from the medical examiner's office," Jack replied. He had no intention of going into too much detail in front of a stranger. "He'll be hanging around for the bulk of the afternoon to keep an eye on things, so everybody should be safe."

"That's good." Max's forehead wrinkled. "Did you tell him about running into the widower in the woods?"

"I did and he has the information." Jack focused his full attention on the newbie. "I'm Jack Harker." He extended his hand. "This is my fiancée Ivy."

"That's the sister I was telling you about," Max offered as the man shook Jack's hand.

"I'm Jeff Portman," the man introduced himself. "I was supposed to be meeting two college friends here for a fishing expedition, but they ran into car trouble and won't be here until tomorrow. It's not a problem for me to extend my trip for a few days longer, but I'm kind of alone until then and with what happened last night ... well ... ."

"You feel nervous," Ivy surmised. "I don't blame you. I think it rattled us all."

"I saw you around where the body was found last night," Jack noted. "You were one of the people questioned by the state troopers."

"I was, although I only walked up on the tail end of things because I was fishing," Jeff volunteered. "I couldn't figure out what was going on at first. I thought it was some sort of fight ... or maybe a joke. Once the state police showed up, I figured out pretty quickly that something serious had gone down. I can't believe that poor woman was murdered."

"We technically don't know that yet," Jack cautioned. "The state police want to be sure. There was a hill. It's possible she tripped in the exact wrong way thanks to the darkness and somehow broke her neck."

"Do you believe that's what happened?"

Jack searched his heart. "No, but I would like to be proven wrong on this one. It's the better outcome for everyone."

"I guess I'm something of a cynic. I'm sure it's the husband. He was acting squirrelly before all this happened. I heard them arguing at their campsite — mine isn't too far away — and he was calling her names and belittling her."

Jack frowned. "That's not what he told us. He said she was the bossy sort. I know from personal experience that bossy women don't put up with being belittled."

"You've got that right," Ivy muttered, earning a smile from Jack. "I would kick you to the curb so fast if you talked down to me."

"I guess it's good I don't do that, huh?" He slung his arm around Ivy's neck.

"Jeff wants to know if we fancy a trip to the river to fish with him," Max volunteered. "I was kind of keen on taking a nap, but we haven't fished at all yet and I would prefer going during daylight hours rather than trying an excursion at night."

Jack immediately balked. "I don't think we should leave the women here and I have a feeling they're not interested in fishing."

"I definitely have no interest in fishing." Ivy's tone was no-nonsense. "There's no reason you guys can't go, though. We'll just hang around here, probably nap and read. We'll be perfectly fine." She looked toward Amy, who was sitting in one of the chairs staring into nothing, for confirmation. The woman already looked as if she was asleep on her feet.

"I don't know." Jack wasn't convinced. "There could be a murderer running around."

"Not one that's going to approach us with people spread out in nearby campsites in the middle of the day," Ivy countered. "Trust me. We'll be perfectly fine. You have nothing to worry about."

"Well ... ." Jack licked his lips and focused on Max. "Are you gung-ho for this?"

"I am." Max bobbed his head. "We'll only be gone a few hours. We might even catch something worth cooking for dinner."

"Well, Trooper Winters is going to be down by the main building," Jack said finally. "Someone really would have to be an idiot to attack in the middle of the day."

"And I'm perfectly capable of taking care of myself," Ivy reminded him. "Go. Have fun. I'll take a long nap and have lots of energy when you get back."

Jack smirked. "See. Now you're talking." He lowered his mouth to hers. "Be careful and aware of your surroundings while we're gone. That's all I ask."

"Consider it done."

Eight

After a two-hour nap, Ivy emerged from the tent to find Amy diligently cleaning the campsite. The woman seemed to be lost in her own head. Ivy didn't expect Jack and Max to return for at least another hour.

"You don't have to do that," she said quickly, moving to Amy's side. "It's already pretty clean and this shouldn't fall on you."

"What? Oh." Amy let loose a low chuckle. "I tend to clean when I'm thinking about something. It's natural for me."

"I wish it was natural for me." Ivy grabbed the kettle and filled it full of water from the gallon jug Jack had retrieved that morning. "I'm the sort of person who is perfectly happy living in filth if it means I don't have to scrub the toilet."

Amy snorted. "My mother was the one who got me into it. There were times when I was a kid that we were running low on money and I didn't know it. They didn't tell me for obvious reasons. She used to clean the house from top to bottom those days. It was only when I got older that I realized what she was really worried about."

"I think that parents believe it's their job to protect children." Ivy carried the kettle to the fire and positioned it to easily grab when the water began to boil. "My parents were the same way. I don't particularly remember them worrying about money – we were relatively lucky on that front – but they would close in and whisper a lot when things were going badly with relatives and health stuff."

"I haven't met your parents yet. Max wants to introduce me but ... I'm kind of nervous."

"I can see that." Ivy offered her a kind smile. "You're the jittery sort, huh? I don't mean that in a bad way or anything. You just seem as if you're always worried, looking over your shoulder and stuff."

"Do I?" Amy looked uncomfortable at the observation. "I don't mean to be. I just ... I've always been this way. Your brother asked me out four times before I accepted. It just takes me a bit of time to get to know people. I mean ... I like people. Sometimes I'm afraid they won't like me, though."

Oddly enough, Ivy understood what she was saying. "When I was a kid, a lot of the other kids bullied me because they thought I was different. It's easy to put up a wall when you think you're constantly going to be attacked."

"Max told me. I think he's worried I'm an introvert or something. He keeps trying to get me to come out of my shell. That's how he puts it anyway."

Ivy snickered. "Max is ... full of life. He's always been that way. He stood up for me when I was a kid, though. He would fight with girls and boys if they came after me. He's a good guy."

"He's a great guy," Amy enthused, her eyes warming at the topic. "Did he tell you how we met?"

"Vaguely. You're a bartender at the place out on the highway, right?"

Amy nodded. "You wouldn't think someone like me could be a bartender because I'm not very outgoing, but I kind of like it. Drunk people are perfectly happy to hold up both ends of a conversation."

"I can see that. Still, how did you end up in Shadow Lake? You came from Minnesota, right? Were you familiar with the area?"

Amy looked taken aback by the question, which made Ivy feel guilty, although she didn't know why. "Oh, well ... it's kind of a weird thing. My parents had a lifelong friend who lived in this area. Her name is Caroline Atwood. We used to visit when I was a kid."

Ivy furrowed her brow. "I think I recognize that name. She lives in a cottage out by the lake, right?"

Amy nodded. "Yes. I've been staying with her. I lost my job at an insurance agency due to cutbacks several months ago. I had no idea what I was going to do. Caroline and I talk regularly and I mentioned what happened and she suggested I move here and get a job. She offered me a room to stay with her and ... well ... it was really my only option."

"Still, that's great." Ivy internally scolded herself for ever thinking Amy was unfriendly. She was simply a woman who had spent her entire adulthood on her own. She was leery of people – and rightfully so – because she understood the inherent dangers of trusting the wrong person. She'd been through a lot. The thing Ivy wanted most was to make her comfortable. "I'm glad you have someone. I'm also glad you found my brother. I think you're going to be good for him."

"Yeah? How so?"

"My brother is loyal ... and fun ... and gregarious ... and the life of the party. He's never been one to settle down before, though. I think my parents had different concerns for us when we were growing up. They worried I would withdraw into myself and Max would spread himself too thin because he likes to share his grace far and wide."

"I can't imagine your parents being worried about you withdrawing. You're very sociable."

"I wasn't always," Ivy admitted. "Jack has been good for me. Actually, I think we've been good for each other. Since we got together I've been more open to social gatherings ... and festivals ... and just living life to the fullest. I think Max can do that for you, too."

"That would be nice." A whimsical, almost sad expression flitted across Amy's face. "I'm just worried that he'll eventually realize I'm boring or too much work and run away."

Ivy didn't want to make a promise she couldn't keep, but she felt relatively certain that Max wasn't going anywhere, especially right now. "Trust in Max. He seems to have legitimate feelings for you. I obviously can't tell you how things are going to go, but I have a good feeling."

"It would be nice if things went well. I could use a win." Amy exhaled heavily and then went back to cleaning. "Do you think they're going to make us eat their fish when they get back? I'm not exactly a fan of fish."

"You don't have to eat anything you don't want to eat," Ivy reassured her. "We have burgers, hot dogs, and even vegetarian fare if you like tofu and protein patties."

"I think I'll stick with the burgers. No offense."

"None taken. It's an acquired taste. Jack doesn't like the protein patties either. He makes gagging noises when he tries to eat them."

"Jack seems like a wonderful man. You guys are obviously happy together."

"We are. I think you and Max are going to be happy together, too."

"It's a little early to make predictions, but I have my fingers crossed."

"I do, too."

THE SUN WAS STARTING TO DESCEND by the time Max and Jack returned. They carried a shared string full of fish and were triumphant when they climbed the hill. Smiles spread across the campground ... until Ivy got a good whiff of her future husband.

"Oh, gross." She pulled back from his embrace and waved her hand in front of her face. "You smell horrible."

"Oh, I love you, too, honey," he drawled, smacking a kiss against her mouth even though she was reticent. "How was your day?"

"I slept for most of the afternoon."

"That's good. That means you'll have energy for the both of us tonight. You might need to do all the work."

"Shut up." Max made a face. "She's still my sister."

"You smell as bad as he does," Amy complained, pinching her nose. "You need to shower ... and burn those clothes ... before coming near me again. I'm serious."

"Do you believe this?" Max rolled his eyes. "We are great fishermen returning from the field of battle. You're supposed to exalt us."

Ivy was having none of that. "For what? You tossed a line in the water and coaxed fish to bite on it. It's not as if you slayed a shark or something."

Max puffed out his chest. "I could slay a shark."

"You're not doing anything until you shower," Ivy shot back, accepting the fish from Jack. "Have these been cleaned? I can't cook them unless they've been gutted and I'm not going to do it."

"I know my woman." His smile was Cheshire Cat-like. "We cleaned them down by the river, left the innards for the wildlife."

"Ugh. Don't say innards."

"What would you prefer I say?"

"I don't know. I guess I would just like to pretend that they magically cleaned themselves." She laid the fish on the table and stared at them for a long beat. "I'll cook them, but I'm not touching their heads."

"That's fine. We'll take care of the heads when we get back." Jack cocked his own head and stared at her for a moment. "Are you okay? Did something happen while I was gone?"

Ivy quickly shook her head. How could she explain to him that she was simply feeling heavy because of the story Amy told her about losing her job and being forced to move to a new environment? The woman had been through a lot. That didn't give Ivy an invitation to wallow, though. "I'm fine. I'm just thinking about the poor fish."

"They're going to be delicious and happy in my stomach," Jack countered. "Can I trust you to cook them without burning them while Max and I run down to the showers to clean up?"

Ivy made an exaggerated face. "Um ... I don't know. Can you?"

He poked her stomach, amused. "Have you cooked fish before?"

"Not since I was a kid and went camping with Max and Dad. I'm pretty sure I can figure it out, though. You guys definitely need to shower if you want to get close to either of us tonight."

"I think of little else than getting close to you." Jack clapped Max on the shoulder. "Come on. Let's leave the women to cook our haul and clean up for them. It's the least we can do since they're handling kitchen duty."

"I think we smell manly," Max lamented.

"I do, too. In fact ... ." Jack forgot what he was going to say and focused on the flurry of activity down the hill. "Look at that."

Ivy forgot she was disgusted by Jack's smell and moved to his side so he could put his arm around her. They were away from the action, but it was very clear what was happening. Three state troopers had joined Winters and were making a beeline for Gordon's campsite.

"They must've gotten confirmation from the medical examiner that it was murder," Ivy said. "I guess that means Gordon is about to be arrested."

Jack ran his hand up and down her back as he watched two officers pull open the tent and reach inside. "That would be my guess."

Gordon looked confused when he was hauled out. He didn't put up a fight – he was vastly outnumbered and it was a moot point – and instead started yelling about how he didn't kill his wife. No one listened as they slapped cuffs on him. At one point, Winters stopped in front of the man and started talking.

"They're reading him his Miranda rights," Jack offered. "He's definitely being arrested."

"That's good, right?" Amy asked, uncertainty wafting through her voice. "That means that he'll be off the street and incapable of hurting anyone else."

"If he's guilty, it's great," Jack agreed.

"Do you not think he's guilty?" Amy looked legitimately curious. "I mean ... do you think it could've been someone else?"

"I don't see how that would work," Jack replied. "Everyone here came with someone. People are watching other people. I think, to get close to her, it had to be someone she knew. I mean ... I guess someone could've blitzed her from behind, but that doesn't feel right to me."

Ivy let loose a sigh as Gordon was pulled to his feet. The man was obviously sobbing. "I kind of believed him. I guess that makes me a sap, huh?"

"I kind of believed him, too," Jack admitted. "It's okay." He pressed his lips to her forehead. "We're going to get cleaned up. I think we should get up early tomorrow and just hit the road as soon as possible so we can get back home."

Ivy was sad at the prospect, but she readily agreed. "This didn't go how we planned, did it?"

"Nope. I still had fun." His eyes were earnest when she met them. "I love spending any time with you that I can. Still ... I'm not sure we should ever camp anywhere but our backyard again. Just something to think about."

She laughed despite herself. "We're going to perfect camping one day. You'll see."

"I'll take your word for it. For now, I'm kind of ready to head home."

That made two of them. Ivy never thought it would happen, but she was officially over camping.

"HOME SWEET HOME."

The next afternoon, Jack dropped the two bags he carried on the living room floor, causing Ivy's spoiled black cat Nicodemus to arch his back and hiss his distaste for the turn of events.

"I missed you, too, grumpy puss," he muttered.

Ivy chuckled as she swept past Jack and scooped the cat into her arms. "Did you miss me?"

As if to prove he was an angel in disguise, Nicodemus rubbed his nose against Ivy's cheek and kissed her while purring maniacally. All the while he leveled his odd yellow eyes on Jack, refusing to blink.

"That thing hates me," Jack muttered as he kicked the door shut and slipped off his shoes. "I don't think I've ever been so happy to be home in my entire life."

"That makes two of us." Ivy carried Nicodemus to the couch and flopped down next to Jack. "I'm sorry things didn't go any better this time." She couldn't help but blame herself. "I don't know why we're so cursed when it comes to camping."

Jack was instantly flooded with guilt. "We're not cursed. I don't like it when you say stuff like that."

Ivy refused to back down. "Last time we went camping one of your friends died, killed by another one of your friends. This time it didn't hit quite so close, but I'm not sure Max will ever get over the way he felt looking down at that body and assuming it was Amy."

"Yeah. I think that jolted all of us. Technically, though, if it hadn't been for a case of mistaken identity, we wouldn't have been involved other than being questioned by the troopers."

"It still counts as bad luck."

"Whatever you say, Ms. Bossy." Jack nuzzled his nose against her cheek and placed a series of smacking kisses along her jawline as she squirmed. "While camping might not be my favorite activity, I do happen to enjoy spending time with you ... so I won there."

"Oh, yeah?" Ivy released Nicodemus, who made a disgusted sound before hopping from the couch to the floor and racing away from them. "We're home earlier than either one of us expected," she noted as she reached for the hem of Jack's T-shirt. "We thought we wouldn't return until late tonight when we initially made our plans."

"We did," he agreed, pulling back so she could tug the shirt off of him. "What would you like to do with our unexpected quiet time?"

"Well, I have an idea." She moved her hand along the scar above his heart. He was shot before moving to Shadow Lake ... by his own partner. That was his cross to bear when he came to town. He used to hate showing his scar to her. Now he didn't even notice.

"You usually have good ideas," he noted, cupping her hand against his chest. He almost lost his heart in the shooting. Literally. It was in pieces when he arrived in town. Somehow, she'd put all the pieces back together, made him whole again. He didn't think it was possible to love anything as much as he loved her. "Why don't you show me this time? I think it will probably lose something in the telling."

Ivy giggled as he moved his hands to her waist and tickled her. Breathless, she kissed him until he joined her in a gasping heap. "Finally something I want to do."

"Right back at you."

Nine

On a normal Monday, Ivy would've hemmed, hawed, and sighed before getting out of bed. This week, she bounced up with a spring in her step and immediately hopped into the shower. Jack was so surprised he remained behind a good twenty minutes. By the time he joined her in the kitchen, she'd already cooked breakfast and was in the middle of a to-do list for the day.

"I see you're ready and raring to go." He pressed a kiss to the top of her head before shuffling to the Keurig. "I can't remember ever seeing you this excited on a Monday."

"I don't think 'excited' is the right word," she countered. "We went to bed at eight last night, though."

"Yes, but I wowed you. It's not as if we went to sleep at eight."

"Fine. We were asleep by nine."

"I think that's a commentary on my prowess," he argued, his eyes flicking to Nicodemus, who looked smug. "You got her to say that, didn't you?"

Ivy rolled her eyes. "That was not a commentary on your prowess. We were simply exhausted. Murder and mayhem will do that to you."

"They certainly will," Jack agreed, selecting a pod from the bin on the counter and slipping it into place. "I thought I would give it a few days and then call Trooper Winters for an update on Gordon."

The conversational shift threw Ivy. "Oh." She touched her tongue to her top lip as she considered the statement. "Have you been thinking about this the whole time?"

"I haven't been thinking about it the whole time. I've been focused on you, in case you forgot."

"How could I forget that? I'm still a-tingle from it."

He snickered. "Very cute." He leaned over and brushed a kiss against her lips. The contact was welcome, although he had no idea why he was so antsy this morning. In truth, he'd slept like the dead and was feeling rested and relaxed. Still, he couldn't shake the nagging feeling that there was something he was supposed to do. "What are your plans for the day, by the way?"

"I plan on working at the nursery with my father," she replied without hesitation. "You haven't really answered my question, though. Don't dodge it now."

"What question did you ask?"

"I asked if you've been thinking about Stacy Shepherd's murder the entire time." She kept her eyes on him, legitimate worry flitting through the blue depths.

"Not the *entire* time," he hedged, sighing when she refused to look away. "I can see you're not going to let this go."

"If the tables were reversed, you wouldn't let it go either."

"Fair enough." He dragged a hand through his dark hair. "The thing is, I'm bothered by a few things. I know it's not my case, but we were still close when it happened. I want to make sure that everything that can be done has happened."

"Do you not trust Trooper Winters? I mean ... he seemed like a nice enough guy and I got the feeling he was diligent. You obviously feel differently, though."

"I don't." Jack fervently shook his head. "I believe he's working to the best of his ability to make sure everything adds up. It's just ... I'm bothered by what happened. I don't understand how nobody saw anything."

Jack had a logical mind. Ivy did for the most part, too. Unlike her fiancé, though, she could imagine exactly how the crime went down. "No one was paying attention, Jack," she noted as she collected her thoughts. "We were caught up in each other. Everyone else at the campground was doing the same thing, focusing on their friends and loved ones. It was all husbands and wives ... and young children ... and people who wanted to frolic. There were even a few older couples, but they were already in bed. People are supposed to be safe at a campground."

Her response only frustrated Jack more. "That's what is truly bothering me," he admitted. "Who goes to a campground to kill someone?"

"Jason Voorhees."

He shot her a withering look. "What real person?"

"You said yourself that it's possible Gordon snapped, killed her, and felt profound remorse after the fact."

"It is possible," he agreed. "The thing is ... well ... it's just that he seemed legitimately gutted. He was confused ... and drunk ... and wallowing ... and crying. Those weren't prepared responses unless he's the best actor I've ever come across. I think he was really feeling those emotions."

"Have you considered that he blacked out and doesn't remember killing her?"

"No. Why? Do you think that's what happened?"

Ivy shrugged. "I don't know. I was careful not to touch him because I didn't want to inadvertently see something that would strip away sleep for two months."

Jack understood right away what she was saying. For the past year, something extremely odd had been happening to Ivy. She'd been developing certain abilities. That included seeing ghosts, getting flashes from the minds of killers, and dream walking with him on a regular basis.

"I'm glad you didn't see it." He grabbed her hand and gave it a squeeze. "I don't want you having to deal with things like that."

"I think seeing things like that is my new norm," she lamented. "I'm just going to have to get used to it. For now, though, I think you should put what happened at the campground behind us. It's not your case and there's literally nothing you can do."

On the surface, Jack agreed with her. For some reason, though, he couldn't get Gordon's morose features out of his mind. Still, she would worry if he didn't at least pretend he was moving on. "I'll do my best, honey." He gave her a sweet kiss. "I can't promise more than that."

"Fair enough. I—" She frowned when someone knocked on the front door. "Who would be up at this hour?"

"I've got it." Jack strode to the door and opened it without checking to see who was on the front porch. Shadow Lake wasn't the sort of place where people were afraid to answer their doors. To absolutely nobody's surprise, Jack's partner Brian Nixon stood on the other side of the threshold ... and he didn't look happy. "Do I even want to know what you're doing here so early?"

Brian shrugged as he stepped inside, offering Ivy a small wave before focusing on Jack. "I just got a call. They found a body discarded on the highway. It looks like it's been there overnight. We have to get out there."

"Well, great." Jack's expression twisted as he carried his coffee mug into the kitchen. "That's exactly how I wanted to start my Monday."

"Sorry to ruin your after-vacation buzz but duty calls." Brian was unnaturally chipper as he watched his partner upend the mug into the sink and kiss Ivy's forehead before sliding behind her.

"It's fine. I'm ready." Jack focused on Ivy. "Have fun at work. How about I bring home dinner?"

"That's fine. Or we can go out."

"I'll text you later." He went back for a full kiss. "Have fun gossiping with your father."

Ivy was taken aback. "Who says we're going to be gossiping?"

"You just spent a weekend with Max's new girlfriend, a woman he hasn't met yet. Your whole day is going to be taken up with gossiping."

Ivy was fairly certain there was an insult hidden beneath the words somewhere, but she was too cheery to look for it. "Call me later and we'll discuss dinner. Make sure you're careful, too. Even death won't be an allowable excuse for missing the wedding."

Jack's expression softened. "There is nothing in this world that will cause me to miss our wedding. Nothing. I want to be married to you more than anything."

"Me, too." She gave him a half-salute. "I'll try to get all the gossiping out of my system before I come home."

"Don't do that." He shook his head. "I want to hear what your father says. I like to gossip, too."

"Good to know."

JACK WAS RIGHT ABOUT MICHAEL MORGAN launching straight into the gossip. Ivy was barely out of her coat before he attacked her with questions.

"So?"

"So ... things around here look pretty good," Ivy replied, opting to torture him for a bit longer. "I guess the business didn't come off the rails while I was gone, huh?"

Michael drew his eyebrows together. "I don't know who taught you to be such a pain in the behind, but it certainly wasn't me. I blame your mother."

"I'm sure you do." Ivy's amusement was obvious as she ran her fingers over the leaves of a hydrangea plant. "Were you guys busy?"

"It was a normal weekend in June," Michael replied dryly. "We were fine. This isn't the first time you've left me in charge. It won't be the last. I don't want to talk about the nursery."

"Oh, really?" Ivy feigned innocence. "What is it that you want to talk about?"

Michael had no shame so he simply blurted it out. "I want to talk about your brother's new girlfriend."

"Amy? She's a lovely woman." Ivy put on a big show of being demure. "I absolutely adored spending time with her."

"Oh, stop that." Michael flicked the ridge of Ivy's ear, causing her to yelp. "Give me the dirt. There must be something wrong with her if your brother is interested."

Ivy would've laughed at the joke if he uttered it before they left on their trip. Given what happened, though, she was more sympathetic to Amy's plight. "You know what? I like her." That was true, Ivy realized. Even though Amy was shy and often reticent, when she looked, Ivy saw a thoughtful woman trying to make her way in a harsh world. There was nothing to dislike about that.

Michael was having none of it. "I'm going to need more than that. I can't remember the last time your brother actually referred to a woman as his girlfriend. This woman must be special. Is she a stripper or something?"

Ivy could see why her father would assume that. Her brother wasn't known for being a good judge of character much of the time. "No. She's a bartender out at that place on the highway."

"A bartender, huh?" Michael rubbed his chin. "Do you think she has other goals besides that?"

Ivy arched a challenging eyebrow. "Does it matter? There's nothing wrong with being a bartender."

"Of course not." Michael made a face. "It's just ... is this a temporary stop? Does she plan to stay here for a bit and then move on? I don't want your brother getting attached to her if she's going to leave. That's only going to exacerbate things."

"Oh." Realization dawned on Ivy. She understood what her father was saying. "I honestly don't know. Her parents were friends with Caroline Atwood. She lives in that cabin out by the lake."

"I know her." Michael bobbed his head. "She's never been married to my knowledge, no children of her own. It's good that Amy is there to take care of her."

"I think they're taking care of each other." Ivy volunteered what little she'd been able to glean from Amy. When she was done, Michael was thoughtful.

"So, basically you're saying that she's painfully shy and your brother seems head-over-heels for her. I don't know how I feel about that."

"It's not just that she's shy," Ivy cautioned. She'd jumped to that conclusion at first, too, and now realized she'd been off the mark. "She's measured. She lost her parents when she was young. I didn't hear an exact age, but I'm pretty sure she was barely twenty when it happened. She didn't have any other family, so that meant she was on her own."

"Even though she was technically an adult that didn't mean she was ready to take care of herself," Michael mused. "She probably had no choice but to get serious quickly."

"She said she had a job at an insurance office and then lost it to layoffs," Ivy volunteered. "She was in trouble before Caroline volunteered to give her a place to stay. She seems profoundly grateful. She also said Max asked her out four times before she agreed."

"Really?" Michael's interest was officially piqued. "When was the last time your brother asked out a woman more than once? If they're not interested, he moves on to the next one right away."

Ivy thought back to the way he reacted when he thought Amy was dead on the ground. "I think there's something different about Amy. He feels it here." Ivy tapped the spot above her heart. "She might be the one for him."

"Well, that will be interesting." Michael's eyes were thoughtful as they locked with those of his only daughter. "Did you feel it there, in your heart I mean, when you met Jack?"

"Sometimes I think Jack somehow touched my soul from the moment we met," she admitted. "I don't know how to explain it. Max is definitely feeling a lot for Amy right now. I don't know if it's going to last, but my gut says she may be the final stop on his dating journey."

Michael grinned at the way she phrased it. "That will be exciting, huh? I kind of hope it's true. I'm ready for grandchildren."

Ivy pinned him with a dour look. "You're not getting grandchildren from Jack and me for a few years."

"I'm fine with that."

Ivy wasn't so sure. Still, she had work to do. "Let's get on it. I want to tell you about the other thing that happened on our trip and it's not nearly as happy as the previous news."

"You've officially made me curious. Let's do it."

"WHERE DID SHE COME FROM?"

Jack crouched next to the broken body that had been tossed in the median of the highway and studied the woman's bruised and battered face with pity.

"She was obviously in a vehicle," Brian replied as he jotted down notes regarding the woman's appearance. "The wallet in the bag found next to her says her name is Becky Morris. She lived three towns over, in Petoskey."

Jack furrowed his brow. "So, she wasn't local."

"Not that I know of." Brian was all business as he moved to the woman's feet and stared at her shoes. "These look like expensive boots. I'll have to do some research. I'm pretty sure I haven't seen this woman before, though. What about you?"

Jack wasn't as sure as his partner. "I don't know," he replied after a beat. "There's something about her that seems familiar. I can't put my finger on it, though."

Brian's eyebrows migrated higher. "Do you think you knew her?"

"Not particularly. I think it's possible I saw her face somewhere, though. Before you ask, I'm not sure where. It's just an odd feeling."

"Well, I'm not sure how she died," Brian admitted, exhaling heavily as he focused on the high ridges of the woman's cheekbones. "She's a bloody mess. I'm not sure if this happened because she was thrown from a moving vehicle or if someone did this to her and then simply tossed her out like the trash."

"I don't know either." Jack moved so he could study the woman's fingernails. "I can't be sure because there's a decent amount of dirt and grime here, but it's possible she got a piece of her killer. This looks like skin under her fingernails."

"We'll make sure to note that for the medical examiner," Brian confirmed. "She's got head contusions, scrapes and bruises all over her body, and what looks to be a broken neck. The odd angle of her head means that something is going on there."

Jack's mind wandered, unbidden, to Stacy Shepherd. "Her neck could've broken when she was pushed out of the vehicle," he noted. "Odds are she wasn't alive for that. I don't think anyone worried about being caught would push a woman out of a car or truck and just assume she was going to die. That's not a given, especially since the speed limit here is sixty-five miles."

"That's enough to kill her," Brian pointed out. "Maybe the goal wasn't to kill her but just to get rid of her. I mean ... I hate to say it ... but it's possible she's a working girl."

Jack lifted his eyes. "You mean a prostitute?" He glanced back toward the body. "She doesn't look like any prostitute I've ever seen and I ran across a fair number during my days in Detroit."

"Country prostitutes are different from city prostitutes," Brian replied without hesitation. "Up here they're meant to look like country girls. That's what keeps them from standing out and getting picked up by law enforcement."

Oddly enough, that made sense to Jack. "So ... you think she was a pro, do you? Does that mean she was with a john, things got rough, and then he pushed her out of a moving vehicle so he wouldn't have to pay her?"

"I'm not saying I'm leaning either way yet," Brian cautioned. "We have to run this woman to see what sort of background we can dig up. I'm just pointing out that prostitutes aren't unheard of in this area and I can see it going down the way you described. Our perp might've simply wanted to get rid of her and thought she would survive the fall."

"Maybe." Jack chewed on his bottom lip as he shifted to look at the woman's other hand. "There are marks on her fingers, a few broken fingernails. She looks to have had a nice manicure before this went down. I'm sure that it's possible those fingernails broke in the fall, but it's also possible they broke during a struggle."

"Are you seeing something I'm not seeing?"

"I don't know what I'm seeing yet." Jack straightened. "I want to run her information. I think we're wasting time circling until we know more about her."

"I agree. We can't do anything until the medical examiner gets here, though, and they're running behind."

"Then we'll wait." Jack was grim as he moved closer to the road to study a few of the spots where she might've hit if she really was shoved from a moving vehicle. "Do you think it's possible for somebody to stop out here in the middle of the night and dump a body without anybody seeing?"

Brian nodded without hesitation. "Absolutely. There's very little traffic on this highway, even during peak periods. If that's what happened, my guess would be that someone had the body covered in the bed of a pickup truck, pulled over by the side of the road and feigned looking at tires or something until he was sure traffic was clear, then dragged her out of the truck and threw her in the ditch. The whole thing wouldn't have taken more than three minutes ... and we've only seen two vehicles since we've been out here."

"Yeah. I noticed that, too." Jack rolled his neck. "We need her background. We can't determine a thing until we know more about her."

Ten

Tracking down information on Becky Morris wasn't as easy as Jack anticipated. Since she lived in a nearby town, he figured he would have to drive over there to interview her friends and family. An alert on his computer changed his opinion.

"Look at this," Brian muttered, shaking his head as he bent over his desk and read the same alert. "There's a BOLO on our dead woman."

"There is." Jack was grim. "She went missing at the St. Ignace rest area yesterday. She was traveling with her husband. They both went into the bathroom and when he came out he headed to the vending machines. When she didn't come find him he assumed she went back to the car ... only she didn't. She disappeared."

Brian rubbed the back of his neck as he shifted from one foot to the other. "What do you think?" he asked finally. "It's possible he made up that story. He could've killed her in the Upper Peninsula and waited until he got down here to dispose of her."

Jack cocked his head to the side, considering. "That doesn't make a lot of sense to me," he said after a beat. "They live in Petoskey. Shadow Lake isn't exactly a convenient stop."

"No. We need to talk to him, though." Brian started typing. "I'm going to update the state police that we have the body and it's likely Becky Morris. Hopefully that will be enough to get the husband redirected here."

"Hopefully we'll luck out," Jack agreed. "Until then, I'm going to start digging into our victim's background. Maybe something will jump out at me."

"I'm going to see what I can get from the trooper who filed the missing person's report. He might have some background for us."

IVY WAS IN THE MIDDLE OF a transplanting project when she heard a familiar voice. She furrowed her brow, shifted from her spot in the middle of her greenhouse, and frowned when her mother strolled through the open door.

Luna Morgan was a handsome woman, one of those people who looked twenty years younger and could entrance a room in three seconds flat. Ivy was close with her mother, got along well with her in fact, but she was also often agitated with her mother's insistence on invading her life.

"What are you doing here?" Ivy blurted out before she thought better about how obnoxious she sounded.

Luna arched an eyebrow and planted her hands on her hips. "And that's a fine 'hello, how are you, mother' to you, too," she drawled.

Ivy made a rueful face. "I wasn't trying to be insulting. I just ... am surprised you're here. I didn't realize you were coming for a visit today. I would've marked it down on my calendar if I knew."

"And I didn't realize that visits from your mother were the sort of things that had to be marked down on a calendar. You learn something new every day."

Ivy scowled. "I can tell you're in a mood. I don't really have time to deal with ... whatever this is. I was thinking perhaps you were here for a specific reason, but now I believe that's not the case because you would've already clobbered me over the head with intent if you had any."

Luna's smile only widened. "That was a very smart sentence, young lady. I'm proud to see that you put your vocabulary to work for you on a regular basis."

"Oh, geez." Ivy rolled her eyes. "You do have an agenda. Whatever it is, I'm not interested. Why don't you go and bother Dad or something? I think he'd appreciate the company."

Luna didn't bother acknowledging the lame attempt to distract her with anything other than a dismissive wave. "So, I hear you had a fun weekend. How is Jack?"

Ivy narrowed her eyes. She sensed trouble. "Jack is lovely. He sends his regards."

"He's always been a friendly and amiable man." Luna's smile was brutally pleasant, which only made Ivy more suspicious. "How did he get along with your brother? I know there was some strife because Jack wanted to spend time alone with you. Did things work out okay, though?"

Ivy had a feeling she knew exactly where her mother was going with this conversation ... and she wasn't happy. "Actually, Jack remained petulant for the bulk of the trip. He wasn't happy about our alone time being taken from us."

"That is terrible. I'm sorry things were so rough on Jack." Luna barreled forward and finally arrived at the real topic she wanted to discuss. "And I believe your brother brought a friend, correct? A girlfriend. He's even referring to her as his girlfriend, something he hasn't done for a long time."

"Yes, I believe he was in high school and trying to talk a certain cheerleader out of her brightly-colored skirt when last he used that term," Ivy agreed. "Mother—"

Luna waved her hand to stop Ivy from talking. "Tell me about her. She must be something special if she's captured your brother's eye and put him off other women entirely."

Ivy really should've seen this coming. She wanted to kick herself for not realizing her mother was going to turn this into a thing. "She's nice, Mom. She's sweet ... and Max dotes on her. She's a little on the quiet side, but I'm guessing she'll start talking about herself more when she feels comfortable with us."

"Hmm. Uh-huh. Do you think she was uncomfortable with you because you're surly or is she really the nervous sort?"

Ivy balked. "I'm not surly."

"Dear, I thought you were going to be alone for the rest of your life until Jack came along. Thankfully, some men find surliness attractive. He's a godsend."

Ivy made a face. "Have you ever considered that Jack is lucky to have found me? He's not perfect either."

Luna's eyes sparkled. "On the contrary. He's perfect for you."

"He definitely is," Ivy agreed after a beat, shaking her head as she returned to her task. "I know why you're here, Mom. You're fishing for information on Amy. Dad did the same this morning, which is probably why you're here because he didn't get a lot out of me."

"I don't appreciate the negative attitude."

"It's not a negative attitude." Ivy's eyes were clear when they locked with her mother's cloudy orbs. "I just don't know what you want to hear. Actually, that's not true." She immediately corrected herself. "I do know what you want to hear. I don't think I can give it to you, though.

"Amy is shy," she continued. "She's a little nervous and jittery, but I don't necessarily blame her for that. She was meeting us for the first time and Jack had attitude because Max took over our trip."

"Perhaps you should talk to Jack about scaring Amy away," Luna suggested. "We don't want the girl to take off and dump Max. He'll have a broken heart."

Ivy exhaled heavily and pinched the bridge of her nose. She was starting to feel a headache coming on. "We definitely don't want that. Max would never recover."

"So, you think she's the one, too. Interesting."

"That was a sarcastic comment, Mom," Ivy countered. "I'm honestly not sure how this will all play out. I like Amy. She *is* nervous, though. I think Max really likes her. In fact, I think Max likes her so much he doesn't know what to do with himself. She's a sweet woman who is trying to get on her feet. I'm not sure, however, how all of this will end."

"It will end with your brother being happy." Luna was matter-of-fact. "You got a happy ending. Max will get one, too."

Ivy was intrigued despite herself. "We're not at the end yet. How do you know I got a happy ending?"

"Can you ever see Jack not making you happy?"

"No."

"Can you see him breaking your heart? Can you see the two of you breaking up? Do you think there's heartache in your future?"

"No. That doesn't mean things will always be perfect."

"Life isn't perfect, dear," Luna reminded her. "You and Jack will go through things together and be absolutely fine. I've known that almost from the beginning. He's your match ... and he'll make you happier than you ever thought possible."

Even though she was agitated with her mother's interruption, Ivy smiled. "I happen to think so, too."

"See. We're on the same page." Luna's smile disappeared almost as fast as it appeared. "Now we need to focus on your brother. He's what's important right now."

"I can't tell you how happy I am to hear that," Ivy drawled. "And two months from my wedding, too."

"Oh, please." Luna offered up a pronounced eye roll. "If I try to stick my nose into your wedding preparations, you'll cut it off. I'm not an idiot. Besides, this is a big deal for Max. You get plenty of attention from your father and me. Now it's his turn."

Ivy was defeated and she knew it so she held out her hands in a placating manner. "Fine. What's your big plan to make sure Max gets his happily ever after?"

"I want to meet her."

"Well, I can't help you there. That's on Max. I think he's nervous to introduce you."

"That's why I want you to host a barbecue and invite her. A relaxed family night is the perfect way to make the introductions."

Ivy wasn't sure Max would agree with that. "And what if they don't want to come?"

"Oh, they'll come." Luna patted Ivy's shoulder and grinned. "They're not going to have a choice on that front."

"I guess I could put something together for next week," Ivy said.

"It shouldn't be too difficult to make the food and pick up some drinks."

"Tomorrow."

Ivy's eyebrows flew up her forehead. "Excuse me?"

"You heard me." Luna had no intention of backing down. "I want the barbecue to be held tomorrow. Make sure you call your brother in the next hour to make him aware. I don't want him to have time to come up with an excuse to weasel out of the event."

Ivy worked her jaw. "Mom, what if I can't host a barbecue tomorrow?"

Luna's expression was dark when she turned it on her daughter. "That's not what you're telling me, is it? You're not too busy to help the brother who has done nothing but give of himself to you since you were born, are you?"

Ivy was trapped and she knew it. "No." She dragged a restless hand through her hair and sighed. "I'll set it up."

Luna was back to smiling. "Good. Personally, I can't wait. I think it's going to be a lovely evening."

"And I think you've lost your marbles but ... why not? Who doesn't love a barbecue?"

"Those are my thoughts exactly."

JACK AND BRIAN RECEIVED notification that Boyd Morris would be arriving at the station before noon. They stood close to the front window as they waited for him, conversing over the tidbits Brian gleaned from the missing person's file.

"It's usually the husband," Jack pointed out. "He might've lied to the responding officers. There are no cameras at rest stops so we can't be sure he was really there."

"There are witnesses," Brian replied. "People saw them get out of their vehicle. There's a dog run at that particular rest area. Three people were walking dogs and apparently Boyd came out yelling for his wife and drew a crowd.

"At first they thought she was in the bathroom, that perhaps she was ill or something," he continued. "There were two women's bathrooms, though. Women went in and checked every stall. She wasn't there.

"There was also a family bathroom that was searched, but they came up empty," he said. "Nobody saw her in the bathroom. Nobody saw her leave the bathroom. Nobody saw anyone leave the lot with her, although I'm doubtful that anyone would watch random people at a rest area that closely."

"Good point," Jack noted, rubbing his chin. "Perhaps she voluntarily left with someone."

"That's possible. Maybe she was having an affair and decided to run away with her boyfriend. I don't see how she would end up dead that quickly if that's the scenario we're playing with, though. Boyd told the troopers that they were tight, had a good marriage, and nobody was having an affair."

"Everyone thinks that," Jack pointed out.

"True, but that doesn't mean he was wrong. Some people simply don't cheat. I would never cheat on my wife, and vice versa. You would never cheat on Ivy and there's no way she would cheat on you."

"I guess." Jack stretched his back to weed out some of the kinks that had formed while he was conducting research on his computer. "I guess we'll find out. This looks like him."

Brian nodded, sadness rolling through him. "That would be my guess, too."

Boyd was a mass of moods when he stormed through the front door. He took a moment to look around, and when his gaze fell on the two police detectives, his eyes filled with fire. "There's been some mistake," he blurted out.

Jack immediately nodded in sympathy. He understood what the man was referring to. "We're waiting for a positive identification from the medical examiner's office. We did find a purse with identification in it close to the body, though. Why don't you come with us into the conference room and we'll show you what we've got?" His voice was calm and soothing.

Apparently Boyd was expecting a fight because he blinked several times in rapid succession and then dumbly nodded. "Okay."

Jack led him to the room that was already set up and indicated a chair at the head of the table. "Have a seat. Would you like some coffee? Perhaps some water or a soda?"

"I want my wife," Boyd snapped angrily, his temper on full display. "She is not the person you found dead this morning. I mean ... she's not. There's no way that's her."

Jack kept his face neutral as he reached for a plastic evidence bag. It was wrapped around the purse they'd found. "Do you recognize this?"

Boyd furrowed his brow as he stared at the item in question. "I ... don't ... know. It's a purse. I didn't pay much attention to her purse. I just ... ."

Jack could tell from the way he reacted that he recognized it. There was no doubt in his mind that the bag belonged to Boyd's wife. "The identification inside belongs to your wife."

"Did you see the body?" Boyd barked out. "I mean ... was it her?"

"We believe it is her," Brian said as he sat in a chair. He knew better than trying to force Boyd to sit. The man was too worked up. If he sat, gave up the frustration fueling him, then he might not want to get up again. Once he accepted the truth, that his wife was gone, the anger would give way to grief and then he would absolutely lose it. "I'm sorry for your loss."

Boyd stared for a long time. "This can't be happening. This has to be a dream or something."

Jack's stomach rolled and he thought about Gordon. He also thought he would wake up to a better world. He was adamant that it would happen. Neither man would be happy on that front.

"Please sit down and tell us what happened," Jack prodded. "We need more information if we're going to find who did this."

"But ... ." Boyd licked his lips and then slid into the chair. His movements were slow, drawn out and heavy. He looked as if the façade he'd been living under for the past few hours was about to crack. "I didn't think I had to worry about her at the rest area. It's a rest area, for crying out loud. I mean ... nothing ever happens at a rest area."

The statistics didn't bear out the statement. Sometimes horrible things happened at rest areas. Jack was certain that Boyd didn't need to hear that right now, though. He was hanging by a thread.

"You were driving from the Upper Peninsula," Jack noted. "Can you tell me where you were coming from? Perhaps someone was following you."

"I don't ... there's no way." He vehemently shook his head. "We were at this campground on the other side of the bridge. It was a state campground."

Jack's blood ran cold. "What? Are you talking about Wagner Falls?"

Boyd nodded dumbly. "I am. Have you heard of it?"

"As a matter of fact, I have." Slowly, Jack tracked his eyes to Brian. "That's where we were this weekend."

"Where who was?" It took Brian a moment to catch up. "Wait ... are you saying Boyd and his wife were at the same campground you were at the past few days?"

"I am." Jack's mind was busy with a myriad of possibilities. "There was a murder at the campground this weekend, too."

"There was," Boyd agreed, narrowing his eyes. "The guy who did it was caught, though. It was the husband."

Brian focused his attention on Jack. "You only told me a little bit about what went down. How involved were you in the investigation?"

"Involved enough that I can track down the trooper in charge and have a conversation," Jack replied. "He was a nice guy. The thing is, I met the widower. I thought he might be innocent before he was arrested. After, I just assumed I'd misjudged him."

"Wait." Boyd held up his hand to get Brian's and Jack's attention. "Are you telling me that the man who killed that woman at the campground this weekend is also the person who killed my wife?"

Jack wasn't sure how to respond. "We can't be certain. It is one heckuva coincidence, though."

"I'm not even sure you really have my wife." Boyd held on to his last shred of hope. "I want to see her for myself."

"We can arrange that." Brian was calm as he bobbed his head. "In fact, I'll arrange it right now. Jack needs to make a few calls. We can resume questioning once those calls are placed and identification has been confirmed."

"It's not going to be her," Boyd assured the older police detective. "She's fine. This is some kind of mistake."

"I hope you're right."

"I *know* I am. There's a way to explain this. I'm sure there is. We just need to figure it out."

"One step at a time," Brian cautioned. "I'll take you to the medical examiner's office first. Jack, I believe you have some calls to make."

"Definitely." Jack was already ten steps ahead of his partner when preparing for what had to come next. "I'll get on that right now."

Eleven

Ivy was still stewing about her mother's insistence on hosting a barbecue when Jack let himself into the cottage that evening. He'd texted to tell her he would be picking up dinner so her stomach let out a lurching growl of excitement when he placed the takeout containers on the table.

"Hungry, honey?" He arched an amused eyebrow.

"I could eat. I skipped lunch."

"How come?" He swooped in and gave her a kiss. His favorite part about coming home was losing himself in her. He had a feeling they'd both had trying days so he was eager to slip into the cocoon they'd made in the home they shared.

"My mother." Ivy said the two words with a sort of viciousness that Jack wasn't accustomed to.

"Do I even want to know?"

"She ambushed me at the nursery today." Ivy figured if she had to be miserable, so did he. To her mind, that was one of the best things about having a life partner. The other half had to equally share in the misery.

"I'm assuming she didn't ambush you with a gun or anything, so that means she wants something else from you." Jack left her to unpack the takeout while he floated over to the cupboards to grab napkins and flatware. "Whatever it is, I'm sure it's not the end of the world."

"She wants me to host a barbecue tomorrow. I already agreed, so if you want me to back out you have to call her. I'm kind of hoping you're looking for a fight because I rolled over and showed her my belly so fast that I'm a bit ashamed."

"She wants you to have a barbecue?" Jack wasn't sure what to make of that. "You're not going to make me eat a meat substitute, are you?"

Ivy shot him a withering look. "Have I ever made you eat a meat substitute?"

"No, but that is my worst nightmare. I mean ... I know you would never leave or hurt me so that's what I'm left with."

Even though she was determined not to, Ivy couldn't stop herself from laughing. "That's your worst nightmare? Me slipping tofu into your steak, huh? I guess if that's our worst problem then we're lucky."

"I got lucky the day I met you." He leaned over and pressed a kiss to her cheek, hoping it would perk her up. "Tell me what's really bothering you."

He had a way of reading her that Ivy often marveled at. "How did you know something else was bothering me?"

"I know you."

She sighed. "My mother wants to meet Amy."

"I figured that's what this was all about."

"She's already convinced that she's the one for Max. I warned her not to get ahead of herself, but she won't listen."

Jack pursed his lips as he regarded her. He liked to think of Ivy as an open book – almost everything that crossed her mind escaped her lips – but she blurred on him a bit right now. "That's not what's bothering you, though. You were raised in a family of busybodies. You had to be expecting this."

"I was. I didn't think she would pin me down my first day back, but I knew it was coming."

"So, what is it?"

"It's just something she said. It didn't even bother me at the time.

It was only after, when I was thinking about it, that it started to chafe."

Now they were getting to the heart of matters. "Tell me."

"Do you think I'm surly?"

Whatever question he was expecting, that wasn't it. Jack immediately opened his mouth to respond but no sound came out.

"You do, don't you?" Ivy turned huffy. "I'm not surly."

He cleared his throat to give himself a moment to decide what to say. "How did this particular avenue of conversation occur? Did she just call you surly out of the blue?"

"No. She said that she was worried I would be alone forever before you came along because of how surly I was. Then she called you a godsend and said it was time for the family to focus on Max for a change instead of me."

Oh, it was multiple things, Jack internally mused. "Well, for starters, you are a bit surly." He didn't back down even when she fixed him with a dark look. "Well, you are, honey. That's the first thing I noticed about you ... after the pink hair and bare feet, I mean. You have a certain attitude."

"I am not surly. I don't like that word."

"Do you prefer curmudgeonly?" Jack only smirked when she lightly smacked his arm. "It's okay to be surly, Ivy. That was your way of protecting yourself. I understand that. You're not surly with me now."

"Do you think that they spent all their time worrying about me to Max's detriment?"

That was the thing really bothering her, Jack realized. She was the sort who would take pride in being surly under different circumstances. What was bothering her was the idea that Max somehow did without because she needed more of her parents' attention.

"I think Max is the older brother, which means he wanted to be strong for them and you." Jack chose his words carefully. "I don't think you needed more than him, or stole anything from him. On the flip side, I can see your parents being worried about you. Isolation isn't always a good thing and you built a wall around yourself."

"Do you think I still have a wall around myself?"

"No. Not with the people who matter, at least." His smile was warm and comforting, like a fuzzy blanket descending over her on a cold winter day. "You weren't closed off, Ivy. You were simply careful. There's nothing wrong with being careful."

"Sometimes I think I wanted to give you my heart from the very first second I saw you. Something whispered in the back of my mind that you were the one. I tried to ignore that voice for a whole five days before giving in, but part of me knew."

"Part of me knew, too." He leaned forward and rested his forehead against hers. "Do you have any idea how much I love you?"

"Probably about half as much as I love you."

"No, it's double."

"Half."

"Double."

"Half."

He heaved out a sigh. "You just have to win, don't you?"

"I have you. I've already won the big prize."

"So sweet." His grin was sloppy when he leaned in for a kiss. "We're going to have to agree to disagree about who loves whom more."

"Fair enough." Ivy forced herself to focus on him. "How did things go with you today? Did you solve your murder?"

He wasn't sure how to respond. What he had to tell her would be difficult ... on multiple levels. "We haven't solved it. Her name is Becky Morris ... and she happened to be at the same campground we were this weekend."

Ivy felt as if the oxygen had been stolen from her lungs. "What? You can't be serious."

Jack was calm as he laid everything out for her. He spoke in measured tones and left nothing out. Other detectives would probably limit the amount of information they shared with their wives and significant others. That wasn't how he operated, though.

"That is unbelievable," she said when he was finished, her mind working a mile a minute. "Does this mean Gordon is innocent?"

Jack smirked. "I wondered how fast it would take you to get there. I don't know what it means. I talked to Trooper Winters today and told him what happened. He's equally flummoxed. Apparently Gordon has lawyered up and isn't talking."

"Are they going to drop charges against him?"

"Not yet. They have no reason to. We don't have proof that the two deaths are linked."

"No, but ... come on. They have to be linked. It's way too much of a coincidence otherwise."

"I happen to agree." Jack shoved the vegetarian wrap and fries he'd gotten her from the diner in her direction. "Eat your dinner before it gets cold. Then there's something I want to talk to you about."

Ivy mechanically grabbed the wrap and took a big bite, her gaze shrewd as she chewed and watched him. She didn't speak again until she swallowed. "You're worried whoever killed Stacy followed us here."

He internally marveled at how quickly she'd worked that out. "I don't know," he replied after a beat. "It's a bit of a leap to assume we're the targets. The body was dumped in the freeway median, so it's possible that someone else is the target and it was a coincidence where she was dropped."

Ivy wasn't sure she believed in coincidences. "Maybe Stacy Shepherd was targeted because she was blond. You said that this Becky Morris was blond, too. Maybe whoever killed them was aiming for Becky the whole time."

"I've considered that, too. We can't completely ignore Stacy in all of this, but we have to focus on Becky. She's our primary concern."

"So what's your next step?"

"I want to go back to the campground."

Her mouth dropped open. "No way. That's like two hours of driving."

"I don't want to drive back." He leveled a serious look in her direction. It was pointed.

"You want to dream walk." She was already nodding when she realized what he had in mind for their evening. They'd done it before to look over a crime scene. It was often helpful to both of them to do it together. "You want to go back to the scene of the first crime."

"I think it's worth a shot. Are you game?"

Ivy nodded without hesitation. "Yeah. I'm as worried about this as you are. I think it's a good idea."

"I'm glad. I was hoping you would see things my way."

"Don't I always see things your way?"

"Actually, very rarely."

"Oh, now you're just whining."

"And you're being surly."

"Keep it up."

His smile turned indulgent. "For the rest of our lives."

Oddly enough, that was good with her. "Let's eat and then take a bath. If we're going to bed early, I need to relax."

"I have a few ideas on that, too."

Ivy had no doubt that was true.

"JACK?"

Ivy was antsy so it took her longer than she estimated to fall asleep. Jack slipped under long before she did, and she worried he would give up waiting for her and leave in a huff. Instead, he was sitting by the bank of the river fishing when she arrived.

"I see you kept yourself busy, huh?" She was amused when her eyes landed on him. "Did you catch anything good?"

"Just you." He discarded the pole on the ground. It was a dream, so he wasn't really littering, and pulled her toward him. "I was starting to get worried you weren't coming."

"I couldn't fall asleep," she admitted, rueful. "The harder I tried, the more difficult it became. Finally, it was the sound of your breathing that did it. I focused on that and then, lo and behold, I dropped off right away."

"It's okay. I know it's difficult to fall asleep when the pressure is on." He linked his fingers with hers. "I want to go back to the night we found Stacy's body. I want to look around again, see what we can see."

"I figured." Ivy lifted her chin as they slipped out of the woods and emerged in the campground they'd only left the day before. "It looks different from this vantage point, doesn't it?"

Jack slid his gaze to her, confused. "What looks different? Are you saying the campground looks different? I thought I did a good job building that while I was waiting for you."

Jack and Ivy had been sharing dreams from almost the start. Weeks after they met, they found themselves taking on leading roles in romantic rendezvous meet-ups. They initially assumed they were partaking in harmless dreams until the truth came out and they realized they were climbing into each other's brains at night. Ivy explained that she believed Jack was calling to her because he was having trouble living with what happened to him, his former murderous partner trying to kill him. They worked together to smooth things over for Jack and, in the process, fell head over heels for each other. Ever since, they'd continued to go on dream adventures, although they'd limited themselves to once or twice a month because they didn't want to become reliant on a fake world when the real world they already lived in was so fulfilling.

"It's not that," Ivy reassured him hurriedly. "It's just ... I guess I didn't realize the woods were so close to the trail from this direction. You would know better, though. You went into the woods so you could head down to the river and fish."

Jack, his brow furrowed, looked back and forth between the trail and the woods. "No, this distance feels right."

"It looks like it's a longer distance when you're standing on the hill," Ivy noted. "I didn't go into the woods at all this trip. Once the body was discovered, that seemed like a stupid idea."

"True." Jack kept his eyes busy on the ground. "Okay, move to the spot where we were standing on the hill," he instructed as he stood on the trail.

Ivy dutifully did as told. There was no danger in this world. It was a place she and Jack had created out of thin air. Nothing could hurt them here. "This is where we were when we realized what we were dealing with," she offered. "It was so dark we could hardly see at all."

"I remember that." Jack rubbed his chin. "Stacy's body was here." As if by magic, the outline of the blonde's body appeared at Jack's feet. "She was facing the woods," he noted. "That's why we believed it was possible she fell. She honestly could've tripped and tumbled face first and landed the way she did. Maybe she really did trip, but it was probably because someone was chasing her. That might explain how she landed ... and if our killer managed to catch her, he could've pressed her to the ground with a foot or something while breaking her neck."

The visual he was painting caused Ivy to swallow hard. She didn't know how he dealt with the images in his head sometimes. She studied the ground on the hill rather than immediately react. "There aren't a lot of rocks or sticks poking out to cause her to trip. I guess, if she was frightened enough, she could've tripped over her own feet. The thing is, if she was being chased, why not scream? We weren't all on top of one another, but we would've heard her scream and come running."

"That's a good point." Jack dragged a restless hand through his hair. "That means it had to be a blitz attack. If she saw her killer coming then she would've alerted. I think you're right on that front." He lifted his eyes so he could stare in the direction of their campsite. "We left the fire going up there. Everyone left their fires going." He turned in a circle and studied the landscape in every direction. "If I was going to kill someone and expected to get away with it, I wouldn't hang around after the fact. I would head to the shadows to hide."

"Unless he wanted to watch everyone's reactions," Ivy argued. "That's possible, right? I mean ... serial killers get off watching. Right now, we happen to believe that he's killed more than one woman. That might not make him a serial killer, but it definitely makes him dangerous."

"Both the women looked alike," Jack noted. "Maybe Stacy really was an accident. Maybe he was looking for Becky the whole time and somehow screwed it up."

"Or maybe they're both substitutes and he's really after someone else. Maybe our killer is triggered by blondes because somewhere in his past, maybe even a long time ago, a blonde did him wrong. Or he believes she did."

"That's actually not a bad theory," Jack mused, shifting from one foot to the other. "I still think it would've been smartest for the killer to hide in the shadows. You've got me thinking, though. Do you remember who rushed out when that woman started screaming after discovering the body?"

"Um ... ." Ivy racked her bran. "We were here." She moved down two feet. "Max was here and I thought he was going to freak out."

"Right." Jack gestured to his right. "Jeff was standing here. He looked really confused because he was by himself and didn't have anyone to tell him what was happening. There were those two other guys who claimed they were on a fishing trip but were really having a weekend together."

Ivy's eyes widened. "You mean the two hot ones who were dressed really well? They were together? I guess I should've seen that coming. They never went anyplace without one another."

"You thought they were hot?" Jack made a face. "I believe I'm the only person you're supposed to think of as attractive."

"Whatever. Like you don't have a thing for Kate Beckinsale."

He drenched himself in faux innocence. "You're the only person I find attractive."

"Lies, lies, lies." She shook her head. "I've seen you watch those *Underworld* movies. You love her in black leather and you know it."

"I have no idea what you're talking about."

Ivy went back to staring at the people who had steadily appeared in the dream. "That's everybody, right? Everybody was in groups except for Jeff."

Jack immediately started shaking his head. "He wasn't supposed to be alone, though. He had friends coming. They were late. He couldn't control that. The next day he came and got us to fish with him even though he didn't know us. He also stayed at the campsite after we left. Everything on his parcel was still set up when we broke ours down."

Ivy hadn't paid that close attention. It didn't surprise her that Jack did. "You should still run a background check on him. You can't rule him out simply because you liked him."

"I have no intention of ruling him out without just cause. He's just not the one I'm leaning toward."

"Who are you leaning toward?"

"I have no idea. Jeff is low on my list, though. A killer wouldn't seek out friends to fish with. It honestly could be anyone. It's not as if we saw everyone who was staying there. We only saw a handful of people."

"Darn us and our isolationist ways," she teased.

"Yeah." He held out his hand to her. "I don't know what else we can do here. I need to stew on this. What do you say we go up to our camp and do what we should've been able to do had your brother not insisted on joining us and have a little frolic under the stars?"

Ivy was amused despite herself. "That wasn't going to happen even if Max didn't come. I wouldn't have risked the people at the other campsite seeing us."

"In my head you would have. I'm sorry."

She snorted, delighted with his cheeky tone. "Well, I guess it doesn't matter for tonight's purposes. No one can see us in the dream but us, so that's all that matters."

"That's exactly what I was thinking. I'll race you to the top of the hill."

Competitive spirit flitted through Ivy's eyes. "You're on."

Twelve

Jack was still struggling with the investigation when he left for work the next morning. Ivy apologized for not being more help, but he waved it off.

"It's not your job to figure this out. I just want you to be careful."

"I'm not blond."

"No, but you were at the campsite. Two blondes is interesting, but it could be a coincidence. Promise me you'll be careful."

"I have no intention of finding trouble," Ivy promised. That was true. She had other things on her mind today. "In fact, I'm going to be dealing with my brother this morning so you have nothing to worry about."

"You're spending the day with Max?" That was news to Jack. "How come?"

"Not the whole day. He hasn't returned my calls about the barbecue, though, so I'm going out there to discuss things in person with him. If he doesn't show up – with Amy in tow – my mother will melt down and keep at it until she gets her way. It's best there's a meeting today so this doesn't drag out for too long."

"Good point."

Ivy took her time showering and cleaning up, but then she forced herself out the door even though she was reticent. The last thing she wanted to do was insert herself into Max's love life. That wasn't generally how she rolled. She didn't have much of a choice in the matter, though, so she figured it was best to rip off the bandage and get to it. She didn't want the specter hanging over her all afternoon so she wanted to take the brother by the horns, so to speak.

Max was in his office, intent on what looked to be his books when she entered without knocking. The Morgan siblings were close – unhealthily so at times – and he didn't look surprised when he glanced up and found her watching him with unreadable eyes.

"Did you miss me already?"

Ivy snorted before sliding into the chair across from his desk. Now that she was here, she felt out of place. "Every moment spent without you is a living hell."

"I know it. I'm glad you can admit it." He went back to looking at his books but could feel her eyes on him. "Are you here for a specific reason, Ivy?" He braced himself for her to start yelling about him taking over her camping trip. He expected that explosion before they left the Upper Peninsula, but it didn't happen because they had other things on their minds when they fled.

"I am." Ivy rubbed her sweaty palms on her jeans. "So, here's the thing ... um ... the thing is ... there's a thing."

Max slowly lifted his eyes and found his sister fidgeting, something she only did when she was feeling agitated. If she was here to yell, she would jump right into it and not feel guilty in the least. "Has something happened?" His mind immediately went to his parents. "Nothing is wrong with Mom and Dad, is it? I haven't seen them since I've been back. I didn't even call."

"Mom and Dad are fine." Ivy internally cursed herself for making him worry. "That's not what this is about. Okay, not entirely. Oh, geez. I'm making an idiot of myself."

"Just tell me why you're here and we'll go from there," he prodded gently.

That sounded like a good idea. "Okay, here's the thing ... Mom stopped by the nursery yesterday. She was full of questions about Amy. She kind of maneuvered me into setting up this barbecue deal tonight so she could meet her. You haven't returned my calls yet, though, so if you and Amy aren't coming Mom is going to totally melt down ... and then punish me."

Max took a long beat to stare dumbly at his sister. "This is about the barbecue?" he queried finally.

Ivy took umbrage with his tone. "You didn't call me back. That's only polite, for the record."

"Oh, geez." He rubbed his forehead, frustrated. "I can't believe that's why you're here." He practically exploded. "I was legitimately worried you were going to tell me something terrible, like Aunt Felicity was sick or Dad had an affair or something. This is about the barbecue? I want to rub your face in the dirt for making me worry like that."

Ivy narrowed her eyes. "Hey, I don't like this any more than you do. I didn't want to be forced into this position. You know Mom has a way about her. She made me do this."

"Well, you can tell Mom that I'm not sure we're up for a barbecue tonight," Max gritted out. "I'll let you know in a few hours, after I talk to Amy and okay it with her. She might not want to go."

Ivy read something in her brother's demeanor that she hadn't picked up on before. He was tense. Unnaturally so, in fact. He looked like a man on the verge of a breakdown. "What's wrong? Did something happen with Amy?"

"Why do you assume something happened with Amy?" Max recognized that his tone was aggressive, but it was too late to adjust it. "Maybe I'm just tired ... or having a bad day ... or annoyed that you interrupted me at my place of business to talk about something mundane. Did you ever consider that?"

Ivy didn't take the words to heart. "You're upset. Why don't you tell me about it?"

Instead of blowing his stack, Max merely shook his head and then dropped it into his hands. "I don't know what's wrong. Heck, technically I don't know that anything is wrong. I have this feeling, though. I don't think things are going to work out how I thought they were."

Ivy was taken aback. "I don't understand. I thought things were so good between you two at the campground. You seemed happy and in love."

"We're not quite at the love stage yet, so don't get ahead of me," he chided. "As for being happy, I thought we were, too. Things seemed okay last night, although she was distracted. This morning, though, she barely wanted to talk to me. She seemed sad when she kissed me goodbye. I think she's going to break up with me."

Ivy had never seen her brother this way before. He was gone over a woman and that wasn't something that happened on a regular basis. He looked close to tears and it tugged on her heartstrings. "Maybe she was just tired." She struggled to come up with an excuse that would make her brother feel better. "Maybe she has PMS or something. I mean ... I don't think that should be used as an excuse and, in fact, I hate it when people ask if I have PMS whenever I'm in a bad mood. Forget I said that."

She took a moment to regroup. "Max, she might just be having a bad day," she offered plaintively. "You can't take everything to heart. If you do that, it will be a self-fulfilling prophecy."

"I guess." He rubbed his forehead. "I really like her."

"I know. I could tell the second you decided to take over our camping trip that you really liked her. It's not like you to try so hard, though."

"Are you saying Jack didn't have to try to get you?" Max was incredulous. "Come on. I saw that play out. He practically fell on his knees to make sure you two would end up together."

That wasn't how Ivy remembered it. "We both gave of ourselves to help the other," she corrected. "We didn't change who we were to fit into some neat little box. We didn't try to make ourselves small to appease the other."

"That's not what I'm doing."

"It seems like that's what you're doing." Ivy leaned forward and forced Max to catch her gaze. "Love is great. It's the best thing ever. Forcing yourself to be a different man so she'll love you is only going to come back to bite you, though. You can't do that, Max.

"You're a great guy and if she doesn't see that ... well ... it's on her," she continued. "I know you don't want to hear that, but you can't keep giving of yourself and getting nothing in return. That's not how a relationship works."

"I know you're right." He looked miserable as he pinched the bridge of his nose. "I can't get her out of my head, though. I just ... there's something about her. I don't know how to explain it."

Ivy didn't know how to explain it either, but she wasn't a fan of what she was seeing. Max was losing himself, and that was the last thing she expected from the man who stood as her right hand for the bulk of his life.

This couldn't be allowed to continue.

IVY WAS FAMILIAR WITH THE lake that Caroline Atwood lived on. She wasn't as familiar with the houses that lined it. It took her three tries to find the correct driveway. She wasn't certain on that one either, until she pulled close to the house and found Amy loading the hatchback of a nondescript Ford Focus. She looked to be in a hurry as she shoved things willy-nilly into the vehicle.

"Max was right about you." Ivy was furious as she slammed the door to her car and stomped in Amy's direction. "He was right. You plan on leaving and not even telling him. I can't believe you're doing this."

Amy was obviously surprised to see Ivy because she kept looking up and down the driveway, as if to ask herself how she missed the woman's approach. "What are you doing here? How did you find me?"

"You told me where you were staying," Ivy reminded her, openly glaring at the laundry basket full of items that Amy was trying to wedge into the back of the car. "How could you do this to my brother?"

Amy made a protesting sound and abandoned the basket. "I'm not trying to hurt your brother. You have no idea about any of this. Mind your own business."

Ivy had no intention of doing that. If this woman was going to leave town and crush her brother's spirits, she was going to do it with an earful of Ivy propelling her. "My brother is sitting in his office right now wondering what he did wrong to make you turn on him. He realizes that something is happening, by the way. He's not an idiot."

"I ... he ... we ... ." Amy worked her jaw but couldn't seem to find the words she was looking for.

"There's no excuse you can utter that will make this better," Ivy warned. "I knew there was something wrong with you from the start. I didn't peg you as the sort of person who would use my brother for what he could give you and then take off this way, but I guess that's on me. I made excuses for you because I thought you were shy. You're evil, not shy."

Amy's eyes were glassy as she absorbed the pointed words. "I'm sorry. You have no idea how sorry I am. This isn't what I wanted."

"Right." Ivy's fury wasn't even remotely abated. "You know what? It doesn't matter. I want you out of here. I'll even help you pack so you can leave quicker. My brother deserves so much more than you."

She stormed to the back of the car and grabbed the laundry basket. "I'll just help you out here. I ... ." The second her fingers brushed against something soft in the basket – she wasn't even sure what it was – her mind was overtaken with angry images. She had no control over the visions as they knocked her for a loop. All she could do was hold on and pray they would end sooner rather than later, because they were beyond ugly.

The first image was of a young girl, Amy as a teenager. She met a boy and they smiled at each other. Little hearts were practically floating over their heads.

The second was Amy getting ready for a dance, probably the prom. The boy met her outside, though, and greeted her with a punch in the stomach because he didn't like her dress. He screamed that it was too revealing.

Next was a vision of the boy promising that he would never hurt her again.

Then Amy getting married ... Amy on her honeymoon ... Amy's head being held under the bathtub water as the same boy, who was now a man, attempted to drown her. Amy giving birth to a baby. Amy throwing herself in front of what looked to be a toddler to protect him. Amy, her face bruised and red, packing up her child and running away in the middle of the night.

The images assaulted Ivy from every direction and she could do nothing but sink to the ground. Otherwise her legs would've gone out from under her and she probably would've hit her head on the way down.

"Oh, geez." Amy knelt next to her, concern lining her face.

"Do you need me to call an ambulance?" Amy didn't look thrilled with the prospect, but she was determined to do the right thing.

Slowly, deliberately, Ivy shook her head. "I'm sorry," she rasped out, taking the tiny blonde by surprise.

"Why are you sorry?" Amy's cheeks flooded with color. "You're not to blame for any of this."

"Maybe not, but I should've been nicer to you." Ivy's eyes filled with tears. "I'm sorry about your husband ... and what happened to you. That's awful."

Amy reared back, stunned disbelief fueling her. "What are you talking about?"

"The man. I saw what he did to you." Ivy saw no reason to lie. She was careful when it came to hiding her abilities – being a witch wasn't something she was ready to broadcast to the world – but she instinctively knew she could trust Amy. The woman had her own set of secrets she was desperate to hide, after all. "You ran in the middle of the night. You have a baby. Or, I guess had." Ivy looked around, confused. "Where is your baby?"

Amy plucked an item from Ivy's hand. Ivy hadn't even realized she was holding the small brown bear. It had a loose eye and a partially-torn ear. It looked well-loved ... and out of place. "He's not a baby any longer. He's five. He's with Caroline. Once I told her what happened, she agreed that I had to get him out of town. She took him and I'm supposed to catch up when I'm certain no one is following me."

Ivy's throat was dry. "You ran from him in the middle of the night. You'd obviously been beaten up. How long did you put up with that?"

"Far too long. I didn't know what else to do, though. I didn't want to move back in with my parents but that was the plan when I found out I was pregnant. Unfortunately, they died before that could come to fruition."

Ivy felt sick to her stomach. "Why didn't you go to the police?"

"Not everyone is as lucky as you. It's not as easy to go to the police as you might think. I was afraid that no one would believe me. I was convinced I somehow did something to deserve it. He convinced me of that ... right up until he started threatening my son. That's when I finally came to my senses because I knew there was no way a toddler deserved what was happening in that house."

"No, definitely not," Ivy agreed. "Have you been on the run ever since?"

"Yes. It wasn't easy at first. I was on my own. We lived in some disgusting hotels. I managed to find a good job in Minnesota, though. That wasn't a lie. I lived there for three years. We kept to ourselves. I got a job at a hotel. They allowed me to keep JJ with me during the day – that's his name, by the way – and it was great ... and then I saw him in the parking lot one day.

"He tried to approach me, pleaded with me to give him another chance," she continued. "He told me he was a changed man, had gone to therapy, and would never put his hands on me again. He was lying, though. I knew that.

"I pretended that I would give it some thought and then I paid one of the kitchen staff members to distract him while JJ and I slipped out of the hotel," she continued. "We ran again. This time to northern Minnesota. There's where I got the job in the insurance office. It wasn't great, but we were surviving. Then I lost my job.

"I was about out of options when I remembered Caroline," she said, swiping at the errant tears that streaked her cheeks. "I called her on a hope and a prayer, told her what was happening, and she welcomed us into her home with open arms. She never once blamed me even though I've brought danger to her doorstep."

"Why are you running now?" That was the part that confused Ivy. "What has you so spooked?"

"Are you kidding? Between the girl at the campground and the one that was found here yesterday, can you really doubt what's happening? I mean ... Jeff was there. He's coming for me. That's why I got JJ out of town right away. I didn't want to give Jeff a chance to find us."

Ivy's heart performed a painful somersault. "Oh, geez. I didn't even recognize him in your memory. He looked different ... but he had the same eyes. I should've seen that."

"He's gone through great pains to change his appearance, I'm sure." Amy was bitter. Ivy couldn't blame her. "I can't stay here. I care about your brother a great deal. You have no idea. Jeff will kill him to get to me, though. He'll kill everybody to get to me. I won't risk the innocent. I can't."

Ivy instinctively reached over and grabbed Amy's arm before she could pull away. "You can't leave. You were meant to come here, to find Max. Heck, you were meant to find me. I'm going to help you."

"I can't put you in danger."

"Believe it or not, I find danger no matter where I go. It's sort of a running joke in my family. I'm going to help you whether you like it or not."

"And how are you going to do that?"

This was the part of the conversation Ivy knew would spook Amy. She had no choice but to tell the truth, though. "We need to call Jack. He'll make sure Jeff doesn't get near you."

Amy immediately started shaking her head. "No. Jeff will kill him, too."

"No, he won't. We're going to work as a team." Ivy was firm. "You need us. You can't keep running forever. That's not a good life for your son and you know it. We need to end this here."

"But ... ." Amy trailed off, uncertain. The picture Ivy painted was a welcome one. She wasn't comfortable putting others in danger, though. "I'm afraid."

"Good. Fear is great when it comes to keeping yourself alive. You can be afraid and strong, though. It's time to be strong. We're not going to let him win. I promise you that."

Thirteen

Jack wasn't familiar with the lake property so it took him a full hour to reach the house. He found Ivy and Amy sitting at the small kitchen table drinking tea when he entered.

"I thought you were just hanging around with your brother and not going on an adventure today," he blurted out when he caught sight of his fiancée.

Ivy made a dismissive motion with her hand. "That was the plan, but Max was upset. He thought Amy wanted to break up with him. I decided to track her down to give her a piece of my mind and then ... well ... I saw things."

"I still don't understand how that works," Amy admitted. "How do you see things?"

"It's a long story." Ivy flicked her eyes to Jack. "It's your buddy Jeff. He's Amy's husband ... and he's evil."

Jack worked his jaw. He had so many questions to ask he didn't know where to start. "Tell me from the beginning," he prodded finally, taking the seat to Ivy's right and fixing his full attention on Amy. "I want to help. I need the whole story if I'm going to do that, though."

Amy wrapped her hands around the mug and nodded, resigned. "I thought I would be able to run forever. I honestly convinced myself of that. I guess that's not the case."

"Running isn't healthy," Ivy reminded her. "You have a son. Don't you want him to have a normal life? Don't you want him to go to school and make friends? You can do that here. All we have to do is find Jeff and then you'll be free."

Amy didn't look convinced. "You don't know him. You don't know what he's capable of."

"That's why you have to tell me." Jack was calm as he rested his hands on the table. "Start at the beginning."

"I was in high school when we met," Amy started, her finger tracing a line over the spoon resting next to her mug. "He was a recent transfer. He was sort of a bad boy. I grew up in Idaho. I'm sure bad boys were different in other areas, but he had this really cool leather coat and people used to talk about him in whispers, as if he did something really bad where he came from.

"I just knew him as the guy who sat next to me in algebra. He seemed to be struggling and I thought he was handsome so I offered to help. He caught on relatively quickly and we had a good time talking. I thought people must've been wrong about him.

"When he asked me out, I couldn't believe it was really happening," she continued. "I wasn't popular like the other girls throwing themselves at him. I wasn't pretty. I was just kind of normal ... and yet he wanted to go out with me anyway. I thought I'd won some big prize. If I knew then what I do now I would've gladly let him flunk."

She took a moment to gather her strength and then carried on. "The first time he hit me was the night of the prom. I'd seen glimpses of his temper before – he would yell a lot if he thought I was flirting with other guys, which I never was – but I thought he just had a bad temper and he would outgrow it. I was naïve.

"Anyway, he was angry at my dress because he thought it showed off too much skin," she explained. "He held it in check in front of my parents, acted perfectly okay, and then punched me in the driveway before we left, when he was sure my parents weren't watching. I couldn't believe what was happening. I thought it had to be a mistake, that I was dreaming it or something."

"That would be a nightmare more than a dream," Jack pointed out.

She nodded. "Yeah. He expected me to go into the prom with him and pretend like nothing was wrong. It was horrible ... and humiliating because I'd been crying and everyone could see that ... and pretty much the worst night of my life until then. Things got worse, though.

"The next day he offered me a half-hearted apology, said he was sorry, and promised it would never happen again. I was an idiot who believed I was in love so I said it was fine. That's on me. My parents didn't raise me to be the sort of person who puts up with that. My father never would've treated my mother that way, although he had something of a temper, too. That's why I thought raised voices were the norm.

"We graduated and I got a job right out of high school. I wanted to go to college like all my friends, but we didn't have a lot of money. I had to save up for it myself. That was the plan, although it never happened.

"Jeff and I were having sex by then and we were always careful ... until there were a series of accidents where we weren't so careful," she continued. "The first *accident* made me nervous but when my period came regularly the next month, I thought it was fine. I went on the pill, or at least I thought I did, and we continued.

"When I turned up pregnant he was ecstatic. I was horrified. I thought my life was over and my plans for college would never happen. I love my son. I don't want you to think otherwise. I just wasn't ready for a baby."

"That's perfectly understandable," Ivy offered. "It's a big deal. That's why Jack and I have been having so many conversations about it."

"Yeah." She rubbed her forehead. "Later – I mean *years* later – he admitted to switching out my pills. It was far too late to do anything about it, though. He never touched me while I was pregnant. He did, however, insist on getting married. Idaho isn't like other states. There's still a stigma if you're an unwed mother. I tried to tell my parents that I wanted to raise the baby alone, but they were having none of it. They didn't know about the way he treated me so they couldn't understand my reticence to get married."

"You got married even though you didn't want to," Ivy noted. "You knew it was a mistake, but you felt trapped."

"That's it exactly." Amy bobbed her head. "I couldn't take care of a baby on my own. I convinced myself of that. I stayed. He didn't hurt me while I was pregnant, like I said. He waited until I was two weeks out from the birth to take out all his frustrations from the past nine months on me. I could barely walk when he was finished."

Jack felt sick to his stomach. "Why did you stay? I understand being afraid, but why not wait until he left for work one day and pack up? Surely your parents would've stood by you."

"They didn't know. I was embarrassed to tell them. I don't think you understand the fear that was coursing through me. I was ashamed. Eventually, though, after a few more beatings, I knew I was in trouble. I told my parents I needed to stay with them a bit because things weren't going well. They agreed. I told Jeff and he melted down. He smacked me around again and then stormed out. I think the only thing that stopped him from killing me that evening was the fact that JJ started crying and he didn't want to take care of him.

"I was almost crippled with pain the next day when I woke up and it only got worse from there," she continued. "The police were at my door. They didn't even bother asking what happened to me. They told me my parents were dead, had somehow rolled their car when driving home because someone pulled out in front of them, and that was it. My plans to run were over because I had nowhere to go."

Jack held up a finger to still her. "Amy, someone pulled out in front of your parents and caused them to roll their vehicle?"

"Yes. They both died in the accident. They never made it to the hospital."

"Did they catch the individual who caused the accident?"

She wrinkled her nose. "I don't know. I never really thought about it. Does it matter?"

"Well, I'm just wondering if Jeff is responsible. You said he beat you and left. Could he have gone there? It's awfully convenient that they died the night before you were leaving."

Amy opened her mouth to shoot down the possibility and then snapped it shut. She'd never given it much thought over the years – she had numerous other things to worry about – but it made sense in a sick way. "Oh, my … ."

"It's not your fault," Ivy reassured her. "You couldn't have known what he was going to do."

"And we don't technically know that he did it," Jack added. "It's just something I would like to explore further."

"Oh, he did it." Tears streamed down Amy's cheeks. "I can't believe I was so blind to that until now. I just … he killed them."

"Then he won't get away with it." Jack was firm as he rested his elbows on the table and snagged Amy's gaze. "Tell me the rest of it."

"There's not much to tell. He beat me whenever the mood struck. It used to be that he claimed he had a reason for doing the things he was doing. He stopped apologizing or making up excuses. The last straw was when JJ accidentally spilled a glass of milk on the floor. Jeff went into a rage and started going after him. I had to throw myself between them to protect my son. That was probably the worst beating he ever gave me. It didn't stop me from running, though."

Jack nodded in understanding. "Did you immediately leave Idaho?"

"Yup. I didn't stop until I was into Montana. I got a cheap hotel and we stayed the night. I'd been saving up money for almost two years at this point. I hid it from him for obvious reasons. I didn't have a lot, but I had enough to get away.

"I thought Minnesota was plenty big," she continued. "I needed to settle in a place where the cost of living wasn't too high. I did a lot of research and settled on Minnesota. Like I told Ivy earlier, I was at one job in Mankato for three years before he showed up. I'm still not sure how he found me.

"I fled the second time to Duluth. I don't know that he found me there. I did lose my job, though, and that's when I called Caroline. She suggested joining her here, and that's what I did. I cut through Wisconsin and the Upper Peninsula and ended up here. That was two months ago."

"Have you been working at the highway bar that entire time?" Jack queried, his mind working hard as he tried to sort things into some semblance of order in his head.

Amy nodded. "Do you think he tracked me down through employment records somehow?"

"You had to turn over your Social Security number to get the job, so it's possible."

Amy's cheeks flooded a ruddy red color. "Um ... not exactly. I used my mother's Social Security number. I thought it was the safest thing. Her middle name was Amy, which was my great-grandmother's name, so they didn't even look twice when I told them I went by my middle name."

Jack nodded. "Okay."

"You're not going to arrest me for identity fraud, are you?"

Ivy answered before he could. "Absolutely not."

"Far be it from me to disagree with my fiancée," Jack said dryly. "I have no interest in arresting you, though. We do, however, need to keep you safe. I'm betting Jeff tracked you through your mother's number. He probably has a service monitoring for both. It's not that expensive."

He rolled his neck and grabbed Ivy's tea without asking to take a sip. When he was done, he'd organized his thoughts enough to continue. "Why didn't you tell us you recognized Jeff at the campground?"

"And what was I supposed to say?" Amy's tone was tinged with bitterness. "Oh, hey, I know you just met me, but my husband is four campsites over. Oh, yeah, did I fail to mention I'm married? I'm married and having a romance with your brother. Aren't I swell?"

"I don't care about that." Jack remained calm in the face of her agitation. "I honestly don't. You've been through a lot. It's not as if you're cheating on your husband because ... well ... he's a jerk. We could've helped you then, though. We might've been able to save Becky Morris, too."

Amy was officially horrified. "Don't put that on me. Please."

"Definitely don't put it on her, Jack," Ivy chided, reaching over to pat the woman's hand. "She's been through enough. This guy has been terrorizing her for years. Although ... huh. I bet that's why he came to our camp to ask you guys to go fishing. He probably wanted to glean information from Max. Did he ask a bunch of questions?"

"Actually, he did," Jack acknowledged, thoughtful. "He asked where we were from, what we did for a living, and made a big show of asking about you guys. He claimed to be separated from his wife, something that hurt him considerably because she got primary custody of their son. He seemed a lot more interested in getting information from Max than me. That makes sense, though."

"And he dropped the bodies as a message," Ivy mused. "Unless ... do you think he thought Stacy was really Amy?"

"No." Amy shook her head. "I went looking for him that night. That's why I volunteered to get the water. I know he saw me. He couldn't have mistaken her for me. That's not how he operates."

"Then he killed her to send a message," Jack noted. "He was there. He didn't run away and hide in the shadows. He was right there when we all arrived."

"I knew when I heard about the woman found in the freeway median that he was here," Amy acknowledged. "The news reports said she was at the same campground as us. Her husband was on television and telling anyone who would listen that someone must've been following him. I knew who it was."

Her response rankled Jack. "You should have told us."

"I was afraid. I thought you would take my son from me and give JJ to him. That's what Jeff always told me would happen. My hands aren't exactly clean here. I did interfere with custody. I did steal my mother's identity. I'm going to do time for that, right?"

Jack stared at her and shook his head. "No, you're not." He was firm. "I wish you'd had the faith to tell us but there's no judge in the world who would punish you for trying to protect your son. I'm not going to do that either."

"Really?" Amy looked so relieved it caused Ivy's heart to roll. "Thank you so much."

"For now, I want you to use my phone and contact Caroline. Tell her to stay in whatever hotel you directed her to meet you at. It's better if your son isn't here right now. Hopefully it won't take us more than twenty-four hours to track down Jeff."

"And what happens when you catch him?" Amy asked, accepting

the phone. "Will I have to go back to Idaho and testify against him? I swore I would never go back there."

"He's got bigger problems. He killed two Michigan women. He'll stand trial for murder here first. If he ever does get back to Idaho, you would be required to testify, but I doubt that will be a concern given the fact that he's facing two life sentences here."

"Good point." Amy clutched the phone to her chest. "Do you really think we'll be able to take him down?"

"I really do." Jack mustered a wan smile. "Make your call. Then I need to get Brian on this and see what we can dig up. I'm betting Jeff isn't far from town. He wouldn't want to risk being too far away from you."

"Thank you." Amy's voice cracked. "I don't know how to thank you for this."

"It's my job ... and you're welcome." Jack winked at her as stood. "Come on, honey, let's give her a moment of privacy. I want to have a talk with you about running wild around the countryside when there's a murderer on the loose."

Ivy's lips curved down. "Hey, I'm a hero today."

"Oh, yeah? Let's argue and see if you still feel that way in twenty minutes."

IT TURNED OUT JACK WAS lying about wanting to pick a fight. He simply wanted to talk to his fiancée without an audience present.

"This is serious," he announced, running his hand over the back of her hair as she frowned. "This guy is a sociopathic nutcase. You have to be very careful until we have him in custody."

"I've got it. I promise to be careful."

"I need you to be *really* careful." He pulled her in for a tight hug. "I don't understand how someone could hurt another individual like that. It's just ... sickening."

"You're a cop," Ivy reminded him. "This is hardly the first time you've seen a human being turn into a monster."

"No. It's still disgusting." He pressed a small kiss to the corner of her mouth. "Once Amy is off the phone, I want you to stick close to her, keep her distracted. You have the barbecue tonight, right? That's good. Everyone will be at the house together. Make sure you have Max meet you there."

Ivy immediately balked. "I can't do that."

Jack cocked a questioning eyebrow. "You can't do that?"

She shook her head, firm. "Amy needs time to tell Max what's going on, to confide in him. I'm not sure now is the time. Max will flip out and turn into Rambo. You know how he tends to go over the edge."

"I do," Jack confirmed. "The thing is, Max is going to be worse if he's cut out of this. He cares about Amy a great deal. He read the situation correctly. He knew there was something different about Amy and his first instinct was to protect her. If he's cut out of this, he'll always second guess himself."

"Is that true?" Ivy was dumbfounded. "If so, that's some backwards male thinking there. The most important thing is keeping Amy safe."

"Max needs to be a part of it."

"I won't force her to tell Max before she's ready. That doesn't seem fair."

"Well, I'm going to leave that up to you. I don't want you two running around town, though. I want you to be observant and watch every shadow. Can you do that for me?"

Ivy nodded without hesitation. "We'll be safe, Jack. I promise."

"Good." He pulled her in for another hug and swayed back and forth. "I'm going to find Jeff. If we're lucky, he doesn't realize Amy told us the truth and still thinks we're buddies. He might think he can use that to his advantage."

"Don't bait him alone," Ivy warned. "Make sure you have Brian with you for backup."

"I have every intention of being smart about this." Jack kissed the tip of her nose. "I've got everything under control."

"Just come back to me."

"Always."

Fourteen

Jack stayed longer than he planned because Brian instructed him to hold tight while he placed a series of calls. He and Ivy helped Amy put the house back together. They unloaded the things that were in the car and worked overtime to keep the woman calm. During that time, Jack watched the two women interact ... and found himself fascinated.

Ivy, who had been convinced Amy was hiding something from virtually the start, was now the woman's biggest champion. She kept close to Amy, constantly murmured words of support, and supplied endless cups of tea to make sure Amy wasn't wallowing. To Jack, it was almost a miraculous turnaround.

"What?" Ivy asked when she caught Jack staring at her. Amy was in the laundry room folding clothes so it was just the two of them.

"You're pretty special," Jack replied without hesitation, tucking a strand of Ivy's hair behind her ear and smiling. "I want to thank whatever gods were looking down on me when I got the job in Shadow Lake. Do you know it was third on my list? I applied to two other departments up here to get away from the city."

Honestly, Ivy didn't know that. "Really? I wonder if we would've met if you'd taken one of those jobs."

"I like to think we would've met regardless. It might've taken longer, though. I happen to think we met at the exact right time. If I'd gone much longer being shut off, I'm not sure I would've been able to open up to you."

"You just said that we were destined to meet. I happen to think we were destined to find this, too. Love finds a way, right?"

"Yeah." He leaned over and pressed a quick kiss to her lips and then straightened. "I'm on duty. I'm not supposed to be kissing women on duty."

"Good to know." She grinned as his phone dinged with an incoming message, watching as he studied the readout with unreadable eyes. "Anything?"

"Actually, we might have something." Jack pushed away from the counter as Amy entered the room. "Have you seen Jeff at all since we returned to Shadow Lake?"

Amy shook her head. "Why?"

"Brian put out a call to all the hotels in the area and got a hit. Apparently Jeff is staying at the Pine Cone Motel."

Ivy's eyes lit with excitement. "Is he there now?"

"I don't know, but I need to head over and see. That means you guys are going to be on your own … and I would prefer it if you weren't here by yourselves even for a few minutes."

Ivy balked. "We're capable of protecting ourselves for five minutes. You don't need to worry about us."

"Yeah, that's not going to happen. You're going to be my wife … and you find a lot of trouble. I believe that means I'm not going to be able to stop myself from worrying about you for the rest of our lives. It goes with the territory."

Ivy heaved out a long-suffering sigh. "I guess you have a point, especially since I'm a little worried about you. Now that I know what Jeff is capable of, I want you to be careful."

"I intend on being careful." Jack was calm, firm. "I still don't want you guys hanging around this place for even a little while. It's too isolated. Can you go back to the cottage? The barbecue is tonight. Maybe you can make potato salad or something."

Amy furrowed her brow. "Potato salad? What does that have to do with catching Jeff?"

"Nothing," Ivy answered dryly. "Jack just loves potato salad."

"I love your potato salad best," he offered. "Just think how happy I'll be if you make it for me."

Ivy rolled her eyes, but it was only for form's sake. The last thing she wanted was Jack worrying about her when he had a murderer to track down. "We'll spend the day at the cottage. I already did all the shopping for the barbecue. It will give Amy and me a chance to bond, right?"

Amy cocked an eyebrow. "I'm kind of worried about bonding with you," she admitted. "I was careful to keep distance between me and everyone I've met since I left Jeff. If I get attached to you, it will make it harder to leave if Jeff shows up. You wouldn't believe how hard the idea of leaving Max was."

"You were still going to do it," Ivy pointed out. "If I hadn't arrived when I did, you would already be gone." As sympathetic as she was to Amy's plight, she didn't like the idea of Max being left in the lurch. "My brother is a good guy. He would've helped. All you had to do was ask."

"I'm well aware of that." Amy managed to remain stoic. "I didn't want to put him at risk, though. If I told him ... well ... he would've gone after Jeff. We both know it."

Ivy did know that, without a shadow of a doubt. "My brother is impulsive," she conceded. "He's also loyal to a fault and doesn't have a death wish. He would've tapped Jack to help him. He wouldn't have run headlong into danger without thinking it through." Even as she said the words, Ivy wasn't sure they were true. "I mean ... he probably wouldn't have done that."

Jack slid her a sidelong look, legitimately amused. "I think it's best the information came out the way it did," he said. "As it stands, there's a good chance we'll be able to catch him before Max will even realize what's happening. Although, I honestly don't know if that's a good or bad thing. Either way, I want you guys out of here ... now."

Ivy knew better than putting up a fight. "We'll lock this place up and head to the cottage."

"You will," Jack agreed. "I'm going to make sure of it. I'll follow you out."

Ivy's eyes lit with suspicion. "If I didn't know better, I would think you don't trust me to follow through on my promise."

"And if I didn't know better, I would think you were baiting me into a fight. That's completely unnecessary at this juncture."

Amy's curious gaze bounced between the couple for several beats and then she shook her head. "Max said you guys got off on challenging each other. I see he was telling the truth. As fun as it is, we don't have time for this. We need to catch Jeff."

Jack nodded in agreement. "We do. I'll make sure you guys are in the car and on the road and then we'll handle the Jeff situation."

"Will you call when you have him?" Ivy queried. "I mean ... just so we know."

"I will." Jack stroked his hand down the back of her hair. "You guys are going to be safe. That's the most important thing. The rest we'll figure out as we go."

"Thank you," Amy offered earnestly, her lower lip quivering. "I don't know how to thank you."

"Amy, this is my job." Jack was grave. "I wish you would've trusted someone sooner. It doesn't matter, though. We won't let Jeff hurt you or your son again. You have my word."

BRIAN WAS WAITING FOR JACK in front of the Pine Cone Motel. As far as lodgings went, it wasn't exactly a sprawling resort hotel with room service and modern amenities. It was more akin to the place where hope went to die, a ramshackle flop that boasted rooms rented by the hour for those who wanted a quick tryst with a prostitute, or rooms rented by the week for those who had no place else to go.

"I was starting to wonder if you got lost on the way," Brian said dryly as his partner exited his vehicle. "I expected you ten minutes ago."

"I had to make sure Ivy and Amy were on the road and heading back to the cottage," Jack replied, not embarrassed in the least that his worries about his fiancée's safety came first. "They're on the way to the house. They've agreed to stay there and cook for the afternoon."

"Cook?"

"We're barbecuing tonight. Luna is insisting on meeting Amy."

"Ah, well, this should be a nice icebreaker. I don't envy that girl having to answer a boatload of questions about her murderous husband the first night she meets Michael and Luna."

"Yeah, well ... I'm not sure that's going to come up tonight." Jack shifted from one foot to the other, clearly uncomfortable. "Ivy has agreed to give Amy time to tell Max when she's comfortable with it. Personally, I would rather everything come out tonight, but Ivy isn't pushing her new buddy."

"They're buddies now, huh? I guess that makes sense."

"It does?" Jack was legitimately puzzled. "How so?"

"Ivy likes to act as a protector. So does Max, for that matter. When she was a kid, Ivy would go out of her way to protect the other kids from bullies. She got in quite a few fights. I remember talking to Luna and Michael at the time and they were worried she was going to get in trouble over it.

"Oddly enough, when those bullies picked on her, she retreated into her own little world," he continued. "She was far more likely to stand up for others than herself. That's why Max stepped in to protect her. He had a much different personality, but they're similar in some ways, too."

"I'm not going to lie," Jack started. "I don't like Max being shut out of this. I think it's going to be worse down the line because he'll feel as if he failed Amy."

"How can he fail her if he doesn't know?"

Jack held out his hands and shrugged. "I don't know. It might be a ridiculous reaction, but I can't shake the feeling that my nose would be out of joint if someone else swooped in and saved Ivy under similar circumstances."

"Ah." Realization dawned on Brian. "I get what you're saying. I kind of agree, too. The thing is, we don't want Max running around half-cocked. He would completely lose it and then we would have two people to search for, not one. It's better if we're the ones who handle this."

Jack believed that was probably true, but he was still reticent. "So, do you know the room number?" He inclined his chin toward the motel. "Is our guy inside?"

"Stan Jurgenson is on the desk. I figured we would talk to him first. We can keep an eye on the room while that's going down. I would rather be prepared than not if he's got an arsenal in there."

Jack nodded. "That makes sense. Let's talk to Stan."

"Just remember you said that with a straight face. Once you talk to Stan, you're going to hope you never have to talk to him again."

"Thanks for the warning."

STAN JURGENSON WAS A SHORT man – he barely cleared five-foot-three – but his gut was so wide it made him look like he was a balloon about to pop. He seemed excited when Brian and Jack made their way into the office.

"I can't believe we had a criminal staying here," he enthused, rubbing his hands together. "That's a big deal. It will probably make the evening news. Do you think the local newscasters will pay for an interview with me?"

Jack made a face. "Why would they pay for an interview with you?" He was beyond confused. "I don't believe that's how it works."

"Oh, you're such a rube." Stan graced him with a pitying look. "Never give away anything for free. That includes information. If you want to get ahead in this world, you have to make sure that people are aware your time is a commodity."

"I knew you would like him," Brian drawled, shaking his head. "You can plot out your rates for the television crews later, Stan. I need information on the guy we talked about earlier. When did he check in?"

Stan checked his ledger. "The night before last. He showed up right when I was about to close the office."

"Wait ... the office isn't open twenty-four hours?" Jack asked.

"No. I'm the only one who can check people in. I have a maid who cleans the rooms and a crew to clear the snow in the winter and handle yard work in the summer. That's it."

"What if someone tries to check in after you've left for the day?"

"Then they're fresh out of luck." Stan was matter-of-fact. "Like I said. My time is valuable. If people want to stay here, they arrive at a reasonable hour."

"And what's a reasonable hour?" Jack thought back to Sunday afternoon. "What time did he arrive?"

"He was here relatively early. I would say about four or so."

"That's several hours after we returned," Jack noted, his mind busy. "I don't think he followed us. We would've noticed that given the limited traffic. He must have left on his own later in the day."

"He knew where you lived," Brian pointed out. "You talked to him, right? You went fishing with him."

Jack wasn't keen on being reminded of that. "We went fishing together," he acknowledged. "He seemed like a normal guy."

"Except he was at a campground alone."

"He had a story for that," Jack protested. "He said his friends were delayed for a day due to vehicle trouble and he was nervous being alone after someone was killed."

"That's convenient. He was the killer and he used fake fear to hang out with you guys. How did Amy react when finding him at your site?"

Jack was taken aback by the question. He hadn't even considered it. "I'm honestly not sure," he replied after a moment's contemplation. "I wasn't there when Amy and Max returned to the site. Ivy and I stayed down at the management office to talk to Trooper Winters for a few minutes. Conversation was already flowing by the time we arrived."

"Was Amy talking to him?"

"I ... no." Jack shook his head. "She didn't say a word to him. I'm certain of that. Max was doing all the talking."

"Probably because Max doesn't pick up on social cues all that well at times," Brian muttered. "He probably didn't notice that she was virtually shrinking in front of him. Amy stayed behind while you guys fished, right?"

"She did. Ivy did, too, though."

"Did Ivy and Amy talk?"

"I think so, although Ivy said she took a nap. I think Amy was keen on a nap, too. We were up late the previous evening because of the body. Everyone was tired and worn out."

"And Amy was probably plotting her escape even then," Brian supplied. "I mean ... think about it. She had to be terrified when she saw him. He was already in place at the campground when you arrived, right?"

"I think so." Jack racked his brain. "I can't honestly be sure, though. I can't remember. We arrived, set up camp, and then took some private couple time apart."

"In other words, you rolled around with Ivy and pouted about Max ruining your romantic vacation. I can just picture that ... and I'm grossed out."

"Get over yourself." Jack was used to his partner's unsolicited grumbling. Brian knew Ivy when she was a child and wasn't always happy to bear witness to Jack and Ivy's interactions because he found them schmaltzy. "That's basically what happened, though. Although ... ." He trailed off, something occurring to him. "Amy saw Jeff within an hour of us landing. I remember that now."

"How?"

"We were in the tent and Ivy opened the window. She was convinced Amy didn't like her because she stuck so close to Max. When we looked out the window, though, Amy was standing on the trail staring at someone. It was Jeff. I didn't put that together before, but it definitely was."

"So, he was there before you," Brian concluded. "The question is: How did he get there before you? How could he possibly know where you were going to be?"

"Maybe it was a coincidence," Jack suggested. "Maybe he was staying at the campsite to save money because he heard Amy was in Michigan and was searching for her and it was just dumb luck."

"That would have to be the biggest bout of dumb luck ever. What are the odds of that happening?"

"I don't know. How could he know where she was going to be, though?"

"I don't know. That's a question we need to ask him." He tapped the front desk to draw Stan's gaze back to them. The hotel proprietor was busy ordering his hair in the mirror. "We need an extra key to Portman's room. We're going in hot."

"No problem." Stan handed over the item in question. "Try not to blow anything up ... or put any holes in the wall. I'd like to rent that room again if I can tonight and that's not going to be easy if you kill him in there."

"You're all heart, Stan," Brian drawled, accepting the key.

"Hey, this guy is a lowlife and I can't stand lowlifes. I don't have any sympathy for him."

"Your whole clientele is lowlifes."

"That's an ugly and untrue thing to say."

"Whatever." Brian rolled his eyes until they landed on Jack. "Are you ready for this? We need to get him in cuffs right away. I'm betting he's armed."

"I'm ready." That was the truth. Jack wanted to put this ugly mess behind them as soon as possible. It was best for everybody involved if they could lock Jeff behind bars and then stand back to let Amy and Max handle their own affairs.

Fifteen

In truth, Jack had cleared more potentially-dangerous hotel rooms than his partner. Brian might've been older, seasoned, but Jack was trained in an area that saw a lot more dangerous characters being taken down.

"I'll take the lead," he announced as he drew his service weapon and ran his hand over the door handle.

Brian's eyebrows drew together. "Why are you taking the lead?"

"Because I've been through my fair share of doors before."

"And you think I haven't?"

"I think you've had less of a need to go through them here." Jack didn't want to offend his partner but understood it would be safer for both of them if he went first. "I promised Ivy I would come home to her tonight."

"You think you won't if I go through first?" Brian wasn't the sort to get offended, but he couldn't help himself. "That's … great. Glad to know you have such faith in me, buddy."

Jack managed to hold back a sigh, but just barely. "If you think I don't have faith in you, you're wrong. You're the best partner I've ever had. Of course, my previous partner plugged me twice in the chest and left me for dead in an alley so you don't have a lot of competition on that front."

Brian's expression darkened. "Is there a specific reason you reminded me of that at this point in time?"

"I'm simply trying to be practical." Jack refused to back down. "I've done this before, multiple times. Have you?"

"I've been through doors before."

"When a potential serial killer might be on the other side? That's what we're dealing with. This guy has killed two women that we know of – the list could be a lot longer in other states – and is potentially on the hook for other murders. He's not going to be taken without a fight."

"If something happens to you ... ."

Jack shook his head, firm. "Nothing is going to happen to me. Do you think I would leave Ivy? That is never going to happen. I still think it's better for both of us if I go first."

"Fair enough." Brian nodded and drew his own weapon. "Let's get this over with. I want this guy in custody."

"You and me both." Jack used his free hand to rap on the door as hard as possible. "Police. Open up." He didn't wait for a response. Instead, he slammed his foot into the door, which gave way with a terrific splintering of wood as it flew inward.

Jack's movements were smooth as he stepped into the room, which was empty. He checked blind spots over both shoulders before moving toward the bathroom. He locked gazes with Brian for an extended period of time and then threw open the bathroom, his gun trained on the inside of the small room.

No one was there.

Jack checked behind the shower curtain to make sure and then lowered his weapon. "He's not here."

"I noticed." Brian moved back into the main room, pulling up short when he saw a pile of photographs sitting on the bed. "What do you think those are?"

"We should check." Jack snapped on a pair of rubber gloves after holstering his weapon and then grabbed the photos. His frown only deepened when he realized what he was looking at. "It's Amy."

"Yeah?" Brian wasn't surprised. "Are they of your camping trip?"

"No." Jack shook his head. "I'm pretty sure that's the bar out on the highway, right?"

Brian accepted the photo Jack handed him and scowled. "Yeah. That's the place."

"And that's Amy." Jack tapped the photograph. "It looks like she's not looking in the direction of whoever took the shot. I very much doubt she knew it was being taken ... or that Jeff took it himself. That place isn't big enough for someone to stay hidden."

"No." Brian was thoughtful as he caught up to what Jack was trying to say. "You think someone tipped him off that she was here, don't you?"

"I don't know." Jack continued to flip through the photos, his lips curving down when he came to a specific one in the stack. Max was in it, and he had his arms around Amy's waist. They stared into each other's eyes in such a way that Jack knew neither one of them realized they were being watched. "I'm wondering if Max is the one who made him come here." Jack held up the photo. "Maybe he had someone following Amy, waiting for the right time to approach her. None of these photos were taken at the lake house ... and there's no little kid in them."

"You think that Jeff wants the boy," Brian mused, rubbing his throat as he considered the statement. "That would make sense. He treated Amy like a dog – no, worse than a dog – but the boy is his son. He's the sort of person who would want to take ownership of his son."

Jack felt sick to his stomach. "He would want to mold JJ to be like him. That's who he is."

"I would agree with you there."

Jack let loose a heavy sigh. "He's not here. We have to find out where he is. He must've registered a vehicle with Stan."

"I don't think Stan follows standard rules when it comes to his guests." Brian's tone was dry. "He just wants the cash."

"Well, we still have to figure out what he's driving." Jack was firm. "I want to see him coming when it's time. I don't like this."

"I don't either." Brian glanced around. "Let's gather all the evidence we can and then go through it back at the cottage. I think we'd both feel better if we checked on Amy and Ivy."

For Jack, that was an understatement. He managed to keep his emotions in check and nod, though. "Yeah. I definitely want to check on them. If Jeff made it this far, knew this much, there's a possibility he managed to suss out the location of the lake house."

"I think he would have photographs of the boy if that were true," Brian replied. "Still, this isn't coming together for me. Jeff needed help to get as far as he did. We need to figure out who that help is ... and if he or she is still in town. That's the only way we're going to be able to keep JJ and Amy safe over the long haul."

"We'll figure it out." Jack was bound and determined that was true. "The only way I can keep Ivy and her brother safe is to find Jeff. They'll both find trouble the longer this drags out. I want it taken care of ... and fast."

"Then we need to sit down and go through this, get Amy's opinion on what he might do. She knows him better than us."

"Which is why she's so terrified."

"We can't change that until we find him, and I think we're going to need her to do it."

"Fair enough." Jack dropped the photographs into a plastic bag and moved to confiscate the computer resting on the second bed. "Let's get on it. There's no way he'll return to this place."

"No. He's probably out there watching us right now, fuming and furious."

"Which means he'll figure out a way to move on Amy that goes around us. We can't let that happen."

"Oh, we're not going to let that happen. This guy has terrorized his last woman. He's a plague on humanity and should be treated as such."

AMY WAS DELIGHTED WHEN Ivy let her into the cottage.

"Oh, wow, look at this place. It's ... magical."

To Ivy, it was simply the house she grew up in. It was so small, Max was moved to the basement when he got older as a child because there were only two rooms on the main floor. Since moving in, Jack had started (and finished) a massive basement remodel and there were now several serviceable rooms in the basement, including a man cave area just for him ... although he rarely used it. He much preferred hanging out with Ivy upstairs, although she figured that might change once they had a few kids and they spent two days in a row trapped in a small house during a snowstorm.

"I like it." Ivy sent Amy a warm smile as she locked the door, making sure to test it before ushering Amy further into the cottage. "This is where Max and I grew up. I bought it from my parents when they decided they wanted to move to a townhouse because it was easier than keeping up on their own yard."

"It's wonderful." Amy ran her fingers over the mantel. "I bet you and Jack spent a lot of snowy days in front of this fireplace over the winter. I've always wanted a fireplace."

"We definitely enjoy a roaring fire. I like to read in front of it, too. Jack is happy just sitting next to me and watching a game."

"Maybe one day I'll get a fireplace, too."

Ivy's heart went out to her. "I'm betting that will happen sooner than you think." She thought of her brother's house, which was small and something of a bachelor pad. "I bet, once things are settled, Max finds a bigger house." She hadn't meant to say it out loud. It was more of an internal muse than anything else. She had a big mouth, though, and the words escaped before she realized her error.

"What?" Amy's eyebrows drew together in puzzlement. "I don't understand. Are you saying that Max will get a house for all of us? You can't be serious."

Actually, Ivy was deathly serious. "He really likes you."

"He doesn't know me. Not really."

"I don't think that's true. You've definitely kept him out of the loop on the big secret but once he finds out, it's actually going to make him feel better. Not about what you went through, of course, but about why he didn't feel you wanted to share information with him. This is a big secret."

"Yeah, but ... I have a child. My son. JJ is the most important thing to me. That's not going to change."

"Of course it's not. Max happens to love kids, though. You're going to be fine on that front. I bet he and JJ bond so fast it will make your head spin." Something occurred to Ivy. "How did you manage to keep Max from finding out about him, though? Didn't Max pick you up at the lake house for dates?"

"No." Amy turned sheepish. "I told him I was nervous about not having my own vehicle so I met him for the first few dates. I wasn't planning on going out with him at all. He was persistent, though. He kept coming in and sitting at the bar so he could talk to me. This went on a full two weeks before he even asked me out ... and then it continued even after he asked me out. It was like a game to him, or at least that's what I told myself."

"Max likes to play games," Ivy acknowledged. "He wouldn't play games like that, though. I know you're afraid to tell him – and I honestly don't blame you – but I think you'll be surprised by his reaction. It will just make him like you more, marvel at how strong you are, and embrace your son right from the get-go.

"It was smart to meet him at restaurants and stuff," she continued. "Keeping your son safe is important and you didn't know him other than to think he was a nice guy who liked to flirt with you. Still, you spent a few nights at his house, didn't you?"

"I did. Caroline thought it was a good idea. I'd never spent a night away from JJ before that. I thought he would have a lot of questions, but he never asked one. Caroline is really good with him."

"I'm glad. I've always thought she was a nice woman. She's safe right now. JJ is safe. That's what you have to keep reminding yourself. Pretty soon, you'll both be safe forever. Jack and Brian will make sure of that."

"I hope so." Amy's expression was wistful. "I'm just afraid that Max is going to turn his back on me because I lied."

"You didn't lie. You just didn't tell him the truth."

"Isn't that the same thing?"

"Not exactly." Ivy internally debated how much she should tell Amy and then decided that the only way to make the woman fully trust her was to open herself up. "Jack and I didn't tell each other the truth the second we met. That took a bit of time."

"It did? See, I would've thought you and Jack were in sync from the start."

"In some ways we were. In others ... well ... it wasn't that easy." She took a deep breath. "Did Max tell you why Jack moved to Shadow Lake?"

Amy looked taken aback by the question. "Um ... I don't think so. He just said that Jack used to be a detective with the Detroit Police Department and got tired of the nonstop crime and violence so he moved here."

"Is that all he said?"

"He also said that you and Jack were like magnets and couldn't stay away from each other and he thought it was weird." Her smile was small and girlish. "He made me laugh when he was reenacting some of the scenes he witnessed. He said Jack was practically panting after you."

"I think it's fair to say that Jack and I were panting after each other," Ivy clarified. "When we met, it was like lightning struck. I knew I was attracted to him, but I fought it because I wasn't really looking for a boyfriend. He felt the exact same way about me."

"That's how I was with Max."

"And yet he chased you." Ivy smiled as she pictured the full-court press her brother must have put on the young woman, wearing her down until she finally agreed to go out with him. "Jack and I both fought it ... until we found out we were sharing dreams."

Amy's face was blank. "I don't understand. What do you mean? You're saying that both of you wanted the same things and then somehow realized it, right?"

Ivy shook her head. "No. That thing I did today, seeing your past when I touched your son's bear, that's only one of the things I can suddenly do. It started with sharing dreams with Jack. I thought it was happening in my head, but it was happening in both our heads."

"No way. How?"

"I still don't know." That was the truth. "Jack called me to him somehow. He was suffering from nightmares. It was the same thing over and over. He was in a dark alley, a man he knew and trusted pulled a gun, and he shot him twice."

Amy was horrified. "What a terrible dream."

"Yeah, except it wasn't a dream. That's what really happened to Jack in Detroit. His partner was dirty and shot him, left him for dead. Jack was stuck in a loop because of it and I sort of helped him along."

"And you were really in the same dreams together?"

Ivy chuckled at the incredulous look on her face. "Yeah. Something slipped one time and we realized it was really happening. Ever since then, we've been together. It seemed somehow kismet."

"That's not what's happening with Max and me, though," Amy countered. "We weren't magically drawn together."

"Weren't you?" Ivy wasn't so sure. "My brother seems to think so. How else do you explain hooking up with him and finding me?" Her smile was broad. "I mean ... other than being an absolute delight, I'm the only one who could've seen what you were really hiding and confronted you. You weren't ready to open up yourself, but the universe realized you needed help. That's why it sent you Max."

Amy had never spent much time thinking about things like that, but she couldn't stop herself from laughing. Ivy sounded so sure of herself. "Do you really believe in destiny? Like ... really and truly?"

Ivy nodded without hesitation. "I believe that Jack and I were always meant to find one another. I think it was supposed to happen this way. He unlocked something inside of me and it's continued to grow over the past year. More than that, though, I unlocked something in him, too. He's my match.

"As for Max, I think there's a reason he was drawn to you from the start," she continued. "I think sometimes two souls recognize each other. I believe there's magic all around us and you and Max happened to meet at the exact right time."

"I care about him a great deal," Amy admitted. "I didn't want to. I planned on keeping him at a distance and making sure he didn't get too close. I failed, though. I found myself looking forward to every visit ... and laughing when we talked on the phone ... and wanting to be near him every moment of the day. I'm still afraid."

"Listen, it's not going to be easy." Ivy's tone was measured. "He's going to have a lot of questions. He's going to ask why you didn't trust him enough to tell him the truth. He's going to be upset for a little bit. He's going to get over it, though.

"My brother is the most easygoing guy out there," she continued. "Sure, he has a few high-maintenance tendencies, but he's one of the best guys I've ever met. You'll see. A year from now, you'll be laughing at the fact that you were so afraid."

"I hope so." She rolled her neck and stared toward the grocery bags on the table. "So, should we start making Jack's potato salad? I get the feeling he's going to be crushed if it's not waiting for him when he gets home."

"That sounds like a plan." Ivy patted her shoulder before moving toward the refrigerator. "We need big pans for the potatoes and eggs. Jack is a fanatic for eggs in his potato salad."

"Is there another way to make it?"

Ivy laughed. "I think you're going to get along with everyone just fine. Don't worry about that. It will all work out. Trust me."

Sixteen

Jack let Brian and himself into the cottage shortly after noon. He picked up takeout for lunch – an apology of sorts for invading the house – and smiled when he caught sight of Ivy and Amy cooking up a storm in the kitchen.

"Are these chunks small enough?" Amy asked, gesturing to a bowl of something she held in her hand.

"That's great." Ivy beamed at her. "Jack is particular about his potato salad eggs. He's kind of a baby that way."

Jack's smile slipped. "Oh, really?" he drawled.

Ivy didn't seem startled to see him. In fact, the look she pointed in his direction was downright mischievous. "Am I wrong?"

"You heard us coming in," Jack noted, placing the takeout bags on the table and moving around it so he could give Ivy a kiss. "You're a snarky little thing, aren't you?" He tapped her chin and grinned. "That smells great, by the way. Is it ready? I brought food for everyone because we need to talk and I didn't want you to get stuck making lunch. I wouldn't mind a sneak preview of tonight, though."

"It's nowhere near done."

"Aw." Jack made a pouty face and looked over Amy's shoulder at the bowl. "It looks like it's almost ready."

"We still have to peel and chop the potatoes, add the dressing, and then stick it in the refrigerator for several hours to chill. You have a long time to wait."

"That's a little disappointing. I guess it will be worth the wait, though." He moved his hand to Ivy's back as he slid his gaze to Amy. "How are you doing?"

"Oh, I'm a nervous wreck," she admitted, carefully placing the bowl on the counter. "I'm afraid to see Max. Ivy called him and told him I would be at the barbecue but ... I feel horrible. This whole thing is such a mess."

"Maybe it's not a mess any longer," Ivy countered, pinning Jack with a questioning look. "Did you find him?"

"He was definitely staying at the Pine Cone Motel," Jack replied, moving to the table to collect a plastic bag. He'd been carrying it with the takeout and looked reticent as he turned back. "He wasn't in the room at the time. We know he's driving a blue Ford pickup truck. We're not sure what year, just that it's an F-150."

"Will that help you find him?" Amy asked, concern etching lines onto her pretty features. "I mean ... can you put one of those all points bulletins out for him?"

"It's already done. His photo has been sent to all the news outlets. We're actively searching. We just don't know where he is at the moment."

"There has to be something you're not telling us," Ivy argued, her eyes narrowing shrewdly. "You're upset about something."

"I don't know that 'upset' is the word I would use," he hedged. "The thing is, I need you to look at some photographs. We found them in Jeff's room. He left his computer behind, too, and we're going to go through that after lunch. These photographs are cause for concern, though."

Amy kept her eyes on Jack for a long beat and then took the plastic bag. Her heart sank into her stomach when she realized what she was looking at. "Oh, my ... how did he get these?"

Ivy abandoned the potato salad preparations and joined her new friend. "Can we take these out of the bag, Jack?"

"Yeah. We've already processed fingerprints on a few. You guys can look at those."

Amy's hands were shaking as she tried to open the bag, but Ivy offered her a helping hand. "Here." Ivy was calm as she removed the stack of photos and immediately handed them to Amy. "When were these taken?"

"I don't know." Jack sank into a chair as Brian started removing containers of food and doling them out. "I was hoping Amy could tell me. You've been here six weeks, right?"

"Eight," she corrected. "I spent two whole weeks hiding in Caroline's house once we arrived. I was paranoid because I was sure he'd somehow followed me."

"We can't be certain until we take him into custody, but I'm willing to bet he figured out you were in Michigan," Jack offered. "I don't think he could find your exact location, though. I think he hired someone to take these photos. That's why he had snapshots printed out instead of on a flash drive or disc. They were sent as tangible proof."

"Who are you thinking?" Ivy asked, legitimately curious. "Who would help him?"

"We've been talking about that," Brian interjected. "The safest bet would be a private investigator. My guess is he was going from region to region to search for her ... unless he was aware of your parents' friendship with Caroline."

Amy immediately started shaking her head. "No. I know I never mentioned her. It's not like we ever had a lot of heart-to-heart talks. The only reason I thought it was safe to flee here is because I was certain he didn't know about her."

"Then he's flying blind and lucked out by finding an investigator who somehow managed to track you down," Brian noted. "The thing is, all those photos are taken in your place of business. None are taken at the lake house ... and none are of your son. Can I ask ... did you take extra precautions when you were leaving the bar after your shift?"

Amy emphatically bobbed her head. "Every night, without fail, I drove twenty miles out of my way and took a roundabout trek to get to the lake house. I know it sounds ridiculous but that's the only way I felt safe."

"It doesn't sound ridiculous at all. I think that's what kept you safe. We need to figure out what private detective he hired. If you can recognize a face, then we can track that individual down and get answers from him."

Amy wiped her wet hands on the seat of her pants. "I can try."

"That's good." Brian pulled his phone out of his pocket. "There are four in the area who are known to advertise. I would assume Jeff would go with one of them because they're the most visible." He showed her a series of photos. In turn, she shook her head. On the third photo, though, she grabbed his phone and brought it closer to her face.

"I recognize him from the bar. He came in at least four or five times while I was there."

Brian took back the phone and stared. "Darren Gibson," he intoned, wrinkling his nose. "I'm not surprised it's him."

Jack was out of the loop. "What do we know about him?"

"He's a jerk," Ivy answered before Brian could. "He's a complete and total jerk. Oh, he's also a pervert, too. He got expelled when we were in high school because he put a secret camera in the girls' changing room and was trying to sell the footage to the other boys in the school."

Jack made a face. "I'm sorry but ... what? Why isn't he in prison?"

"Because his parents pleaded that he was a good kid who just got caught up in some terrible hormonal imbalance," Brian replied. "I pushed for him to be prosecuted but lost. He got away with it. He was a slacker, though, and never amounted to anything. Being a PI was basically the only option he had."

"Are you going to track him down?" Ivy asked.

"He doesn't have an office," Brian pointed out. "He works out of his car most of the time. I'm going to send a uniform over to his house, but I doubt he'll be there. He's a paranoid little turd. We can call him, but he won't return the calls. We're going to need to track him down on the road, and that won't be easy."

"I don't understand how he doesn't have an office," Jack

complained. "Who can be in the service industry like this and not have an office to meet clients at?"

"The sort of clients he takes on are the types that are perfectly happy meeting at a strip club or bar," Brian answered. "He's not helping anyone with any high-class problems."

"That sounds exactly like the sort of person Jeff would hire," Amy confirmed. "The sleazier the better in his book. He would especially like someone who was willing to work outside of ethical lines."

"And that describes Darren to a tee," Brian said grimly. "We're going to have to put out a notice on the state police band to see if they stumble across him, too. I don't know that we'll luck out, but we have to try."

Jack accepted the burger container Brian handed him and motioned for Amy to sit down. She looked to be lost in her own little world but acquiesced. She wordlessly took the container Brian handed her but didn't open it.

"Did Darren ever say anything to you when he was in the bar?" Jack asked. "I mean ... did he try to get personal information from you?"

"No more than anyone else," Amy replied. "Most of the guys who came in flirted with me. I figured that was part of the job, though. Drunk guys think they're so adorable that no one could ever turn them down.

"I ignored almost all of them and just smiled and served another drink when they asked," she continued. "The only one I paid attention to was Max ... and that was because he was different."

"Different how?"

"He didn't spend all his time staring at my butt and boobs. I mean ... I'm sure he checked them out once or twice. When we were talking, though, he was always focused on my face. He actually listened, although I made a point not to tell him anything."

"I'm betting Darren tried to follow you from the bar more than once," Jack said. "He probably even tried to figure out who you were staying with. Did you tell anyone who you were associated with in town?"

"No. Only Max, and that was a good week and a half after we started dating. It kind of slipped out. I warned him not to tell anyone, although I lied and said it was because I didn't want guys from the bar following me home and hitting on me. He seemed to understand."

"That sounds like Max," Jack agreed, rubbing the back of his neck. "Basically, I think Darren delivered the photos to Jeff and told him where to start looking for you. He might've even been aware that you were going camping with Max. Did that information come out at work?"

Amy nodded, thoughtful. "I had to ask my boss for the weekend off. He didn't give me any grief about it. A lot of the regulars teased me for going on a weekend trip with Max, though. Everyone there knew ... although I'm not sure how they figured out what campground we were going to."

"That wouldn't have been hard to suss out," Brian said. "Ivy and Jack weren't keeping it a secret. I knew ... Michael and Luna knew ... half the people in town knew. Heck, Ava knew because she kept trying to talk Jack out of going camping."

Now it was Ivy's turn to make a face. "And why is that?"

"Because she wanted him to warm her sleeping bag instead of yours," Brian replied, not missing a beat. "Get over it. She throws herself at Jack on a regular basis. He, however, is devoted to you and doesn't give her the time of day."

"I'm a good fiancé," Jack agreed, smirking as he shoved a fry in Ivy's mouth to make sure she didn't go off on a tangent. "That's not important now, though. Brian is right. Finding out which campground we were going to wouldn't have been difficult. The question is: Why would Jeff bother going there? I mean ... did he think you would have JJ with you? If so, he might've thought he had a chance to grab the kid and run when no one was looking."

"There was no JJ, though," Ivy pointed out. "He wasn't there. Why stick around? Why kill Stacy and Becky?"

"I'm still on the fence whether or not he realized that Stacy wasn't Amy," Jack admitted. "The hair was similar enough that it convinced us she was the victim even though we didn't see a face. He could've killed her in a fit of rage because he thought she was Amy ... or he could've killed her as a message to Amy."

"Which do you think?" Brian asked.

"I don't know." Amy's voice cracked. "I feel he knew it wasn't me, but I don't know that it matters. Either way, she's dead because of me. The other girl, too. I caused all of this."

"You didn't." Jack was firm. "This is not your fault. Jeff is the sicko. This is his fault. He's the reason all of this happened."

"I can't help thinking that I'm to blame." Amy's lower lip trembled. "Those women would still be alive if Jeff wasn't searching for me."

"You didn't kill them, though." Jack refused to back down. "You were a victim in all of this. You can't blame yourself. All we can do is move forward, and that's exactly what we plan to do. We're not going to stop until he's in custody and you're safe. You have my word."

Gratitude reared up and gripped Amy by the throat. "Thank you. You've gone above and beyond."

"Not until we catch him we haven't," Brian argued. "Once that happens, I think there are a lot of people who will want to get in line to question him. I doubt that Stacy and Becky were his first victims. I'm sure there were more."

"I think you can count on that," Jack agreed. "Let's start digging, shall we?"

IT WAS ALMOST FIVE BEFORE THEY packed up the photos and computer and moved it to the bedroom so prying eyes wouldn't catch on that there was trouble. Ivy allowed Amy to freshen up in her bathroom and helped Jack scour the room to make sure they hadn't left any clues out for her parents or brother to find.

"What do you think?" she asked, nervously gnawing on her bottom lip. "Do you think you'll catch him soon? She can't go back to that lake house until you do and I don't think it's safe to allow Max to wander around without knowing that there's an enemy ready to move on him."

Jack made an exaggerated face. "You're the one who said it was up to Amy to tell Max what was going on."

"And I stand by that."

"You just said he needs to know."

"He does." Ivy was unflappable. "I'm hoping Amy gets up the gumption to tell him tonight ... after she meets my parents and gets run through the gauntlet, of course. The sooner she tells him, the better. She still has to make the decision herself."

"So ... how does that play into what you just said?" Jack pressed. "If you're worried about Max – and I think you have a right to be because I'm sure Jeff has done his research when it comes to the man sleeping with his wife – then we have to warn him."

"Or we could just arrange it so they both get really drunk and have to stay in the extra bedroom downstairs."

Jack's mouth dropped open. "You cannot be serious."

"Oh, I'm serious. The best way to keep Max safe is to force him to spend the night here."

"Only you would think that's a legitimate possibility."

"What's wrong with that idea? I'll just keep serving him beer all night and Amy can pretend she's drunk, too. They'll be under this roof tonight. There's safety in numbers. You can't argue with that."

He was incredulous. "I most certainly can. Your brother has to know the truth. I know you don't want to push Amy into doing something she's not ready to do, but this isn't a normal situation. Your brother could get hurt if he doesn't understand what he's up against. I know you don't want that."

Ivy definitely didn't want that. "No, I don't. It's just ... she's not ready."

"I don't think that matters now." Jack was matter-of-fact. "This is bigger than any one of us. We're all involved. Max is going to have to be told the truth whether you like it or not, whether Amy is ready or not."

Ivy made a protesting sound, but she didn't get a chance to argue because Amy picked that moment to appear in the room. Her eyes were clear, her blond hair brushed and ordered, and the smile she sent Ivy was small, heartfelt, and resigned.

"He's right," she said, her voice strong and clear. "Max has to know. I plan to tell him tonight."

"You do?" Ivy was relieved despite herself. "I didn't think you were there yet."

"I'm not. In fact, it's the last thing I want to do. I'm afraid that the moment I tell him he's going to be out the door and running as fast as he can in the opposite direction. That's something I don't want to deal with … but I have to.

"Do you know what's worse than your brother leaving me?" she continued. "Losing him for another reason. Jeff won't hesitate to kill him. I'm actually surprised he didn't try to make a move when you all went off fishing."

"Why didn't you tell us then?" Jack asked. "You could've warned us and it all would've been over in seconds."

"I was so shocked to see him at the site that I didn't know what to do. I was terrified … and for more than one reason. I thought he might be armed. I thought you guys wouldn't believe me because I hadn't spoken up sooner. That's one of the things that he drilled into my head. People wouldn't believe me because I had a chance early on to tell and I never did. Part of me believed that was true. Now that I know you better, I see that I was mistaken. I was too afraid in the moment to do anything, though."

Ivy took pity on her. "It's going to be okay. We're going to figure it out. Are you sure you want to tell Max tonight? I think getting him bombed is an easy solution."

Amy let loose one of her patented giggles and rubbed her forehead. "I think it's time. It's better he knows now, even if he wants to leave. I know that's a possibility. Heck, it's probable he'll do that. If he doesn't, though, it will be a nice surprise. At least this way I know Jeff won't be able to fool him into thinking they're friends and get at him that way. I can't allow that to happen."

"You can't," Jack agreed, secretly relieved. "Here's the thing: I think you should keep it to yourself as long as Luna and Michael are here. They're going to be all over you as it is, so I think you should just get through dinner. Then we'll find a way to maneuver them out of the house and leave you and Max to talk in private. We'll take a walk in the woods or something."

"I think that sounds like a smart plan," Ivy said. "My parents are going to be gushing over you, but once the novelty of meeting you fades, they'll leave without complaint. Once they're gone, then you'll have your moment. How does that sound?"

"Terrifying. It's the right thing to do, though."

"It really is. I'm glad you've come to this decision. I'll be here to help you after the fact if you need it."

"I appreciate it. I'll never be able to repay what you've done for me."

"You don't have to repay anything. It was the right thing to do. Now, let's check all the food and make sure that's ready so we can get dinner on the table promptly. I'm guessing my parents will be early."

"There's something to look forward to."

"You don't even know the half of it."

Seventeen

Max was through the door without knocking a full thirty minutes early. Ivy wasn't surprised to see him. She expected him to come up with a reason for an early arrival ... especially when he heard Amy was helping Ivy with the food.

"I brought pie." He shoved a store-bought pie into Ivy's hands without looking at her. "It's blueberry. You like blueberries."

Ivy cocked an eyebrow. "I do like blueberries," she confirmed, slapping the pie into Jack's hands when she noticed Max was starting to track his girlfriend across the room. "Come here." She snagged him by the back of the shirt and yanked him back before he could escape in Amy's direction. "Don't go over there and smother her."

Max drew his eyebrows together, his agitation obvious. "Is that what she said? Does she think I'm smothering her?"

Despite Max's annoying tendencies – and at least three were on display now – Ivy felt sorry for him. "She didn't say anything," Ivy hissed, keeping her voice low. "She just hung out all afternoon and we cooked and got to know one another. You need to chill out."

"But ... I was sure she was about to break up with me," Max admitted. "Now she's here. I'm happy about that, don't get me wrong, but I want to make sure she's comfortable. I wasn't expecting this."

Ivy was loyal to her brother ... sometimes to a fault. She wanted to tell him what was going on because she was certain he would smooth over Amy's frayed feelings in a matter of seconds. She knew better than that, though. This wasn't her fight.

"It's going to be fine." She rested her hand on his shoulder and stared directly into his eyes. "I promise this is going to be okay. You need to calm down, though. You're acting weird. With Mom and Dad coming over, that's the last thing you need."

He heaved out a sigh. He wanted to push things further. Deep down, though, he knew Ivy was right. "I'll try to be good."

"That would be best. Now, go over there and greet her like a normal person. Give her a kiss and a hug but don't pounce on her as if she's dessert. You brought a different dessert. Try to remember that."

"I'm on it." Max offered her a mock salute and then turned on his heel. He was obviously happy to be free of his sister so he could join the person he really wanted to spend time with.

"This is going to be a long night," Jack murmured as he moved to her side. "Is it wrong that I'm looking forward to your parents leaving before they even get here?"

"No. That's basically how I live my life."

"Good to know."

BY THE TIME MICHAEL AND LUNA arrived, Amy had managed to wrestle control of her emotions. She wasn't ready to jump out of her skin every time Max made a move toward her and she actually managed a few smiles that weren't nervous reactions and nothing more. She kept telling herself that everything was going to be okay ... even though she wasn't entirely sure that was true. She opted to have faith in Ivy. She figured the woman knew Max better than anyone. She wanted to believe things would be okay, so that's what she told herself.

"You are just adorable," Luna announced as she crossed Ivy's living room – ignoring her daughter and Jack in the process – and lasered in on the diminutive blonde. "I can see why Max tripped over himself to get to you. You're so cute I want to put you into my pocket."

Ivy furrowed her brow as Amy worked her jaw. "Mom, I don't think that's a normal thing to say to a person you've just met. You want to put her in your pocket? What does that even mean?"

"That's a very good question," Max drawled, shaking his head. "I want to know what that means, too."

"It means that she's the cutest thing I've ever seen," Luna snapped, fixing her offspring with quelling looks in turn. "Now, if you will excuse me, I'm talking to Amy. How do you feel about my son?"

Amy looked like a deer caught in headlights as she worked her jaw. "Oh, um … ."

"Geez, Mom," Ivy complained. "Why don't you ask her what her favorite color is first or something. You know, ease into it."

Luna made an exaggerated face. "I'm talking to Amy. Why don't you mind your own business, huh? Don't you have a fiancé who is in desperate need of some attention?"

"Definitely." Jack bobbed his head without hesitation and slipped a finger through the belt loop on Ivy's capris. "In fact, we're going to be over here so she can give me a lot of attention."

"That sounds like a great idea."

Ivy fought the effort, but Jack was firm as he dragged her away. "We have to help Amy," Ivy hissed.

"No, we don't." Jack shook his head and tapped the end of her nose to keep her eyes on him. "Amy is a big girl. She's dealt with worse than this. She'll be fine."

"Don't you think she's already dealing with enough?"

"Yes, which is why it's good for your parents to distract her." Jack refused to back down, instead tugging Ivy into his arms so he could hug her and sway back and forth. "Now … just pipe down. I want to spend a bit of time with you before I'm forced to run out, because you know that's happening."

Ivy tilted her head to stare into his eyes. Brian left not long before Max arrived. He didn't want to explain his presence even though he'd been invited for dinner. He promised to call Jack the second they had a lead on Jeff. Everyone was on pins and needles waiting for word.

Nothing had come through yet.

"I guess I could spend some time with you." Ivy planted her chin on his chest. "Thank you for being so helpful today," she whispered. "I don't know what I would've done without you."

His eyebrows migrated up his forehead. "Did you expect me to abandon you? I'm not sure what that says about my reputation if you did."

"I didn't expect that," she said hurriedly. "It's just ... you could've yelled. You could've flapped your arms and did that bird thing you do because she didn't call the police sooner. I could tell you kind of wanted to do that."

His lips curved. "I don't flap my arms and do a bird thing."

"You do when you're annoyed. Trust me. I've seen it."

"Because you annoy me?"

"Every chance I get." Ivy's grin was impish. "I like to annoy you because then we can make up more often."

"Making up is grand," he agreed, resting his forehead on hers. "How about we set a special date to make up once this is all over with? I'll even haul all the camping stuff into the woods and we can spend a night under the stars near your fairy ring."

Ivy's eyes widened. "You would seriously do that?"

"Of course I would. It sounds more fun than driving two hours to camp. That's your favorite place. The odds of us finding anything other than a ghost witch out there are slim. I think it's a fabulous idea."

"Oh, that's sweet." She threw her arms around his neck and pressed her cheek to his. "I think that's a great idea to solve our camping conundrum. We can do it ... but only for a night and close to home."

He moved his hands up and down her slim back and chuckled. "That sounds like the perfect evening to me." He rested his cheek against the top of her head and shifted his eyes to the living room, to where Max, Amy, Luna, and Michael were all standing ... and staring. "What?" Instinctively he glanced around. "Is something wrong?"

"No." Luna's smile was enigmatic. "You guys are just in your own little world sometimes. I think it's fantastic."

"Yes, I think it's fantastic, too," Max drawled, his arm slung around Amy's slim shoulders. Obviously things were going well at the family meet-and-greet. "We're hungry. How close are we to dinner?"

Ivy shot her brother a dirty look. "Very close, you big whiner. Jack just needs to grill the meat. Everything else is ready."

"I guess I'll get on that." Jack pressed a kiss to Ivy's forehead and then pulled away. "We got steaks for everybody but our two vegetarians. Ivy has soy patties for the two of you."

"I'll help you grill," Max offered. "That's man's work and you'll probably need help because you're bad at it."

Jack narrowed his eyes to dangerous slits. "Do you think you're funny?"

"Most people find me hilarious."

"I think you've been sold a bad bill of goods."

"And I think you're going to need my help." Max puffed out his chest. He was clearly in a bad mood. "Now, let's do the dance of men and grill the meat. I wasn't lying when I said I was starving."

"Yeah, yeah, yeah." He offered up a dismissive wave. "We'll start dinner to make sure you're happy."

Max's smile was serene. "That's all I ask."

IVY AND AMY TOOK ADVANTAGE of a few private moments to touch base while the rest of the family was outside.

"Are you doing okay?" Ivy asked as she looked the woman up and down. "You look okay. I was afraid Max was going to suffocate you he was hugging so hard."

"He can't help himself. He's fearful that I'm pulling away from him."

"You were pulling away from him," Ivy pointed out. "You were going to take off and run, not even say goodbye to him."

Amy frowned. "I don't particularly like being reminded of that. It's true, though. I was going to run away. I thought that was best for him."

"For the record, that's never the answer." Ivy wasn't keen on chastising the jittery mother, but she didn't want to completely let her off the hook either. "Running should be a last resort. I get that you were afraid and you did what was necessary for your son. You would've crushed Max in the process, though. I hope you know that."

"I do know that." Amy rolled her neck as she grabbed a vegetable tray from the refrigerator. "Can I take this out? I think Max is going to keep whining if he doesn't have something to munch on."

"That's a good idea," Ivy encouraged. "Also, don't spend the entire night dwelling on what's to come. I know it's human nature to worry that you're going to lose people when you open yourself up and allow them inside your heart. You can't help but fear that you're going to lose what you have. In this particular case, though, I don't believe that's going to happen. I think things are only going to get better."

"I think so, too." Amy's smile was small but heartfelt. "Thank you for everything. As for food, is there anything else that needs to go out?"

Ivy cocked her head, considering. She liked making mental lists and she'd been checking off the one inside her head all afternoon. "Actually, Jack moved the cooler to the front porch. He was going to take it around back before my parents arrived, but they were early. I need to grab it and take it around. You don't have to go with me, though."

"Oh, that's fine." Amy seemed almost lighter as she lifted the tray. "We can go together. I like spending time with you. Your mind is ... soothing. I don't know how else to describe it."

Ivy snorted at the compliment and yet it made her feel good all the same. She was in her own little world when she pulled open the front door ... and then everything changed.

Amy gasped when she recognized the man standing on the other side. Jeff didn't seem surprised in the least, though.

"I've been looking for you," he hissed, his voice dangerously cold. "We have a few things to talk about."

Ivy forgot all about the cooler and shoved hard at Jeff, allowing instinct to take over. "You're not supposed to be here. In fact, you're in big trouble. The cops are looking for you." She opened her mouth to scream for help, but Jeff recognized right away what she was going to do and slammed his fist into her face before a sound could escape, causing her eyes to roll back in her head as she hit the ground with a sickening thud.

"What are you doing?" Amy slapped at his hands and opened her mouth to call for help. "I'm not going to just let you do this. Not again."

"Wanna bet?" Jeff's eyes filled with fire. You were stupid to think you could get away. I was never going to allow that." He slapped his hand over her mouth and grabbed her by the hair. "We have a lot of things to talk about, including my son. We need to get away from this place first, though. We don't want your new boyfriend trying to play hero, right? Let's get out of here, dear. I've missed you so much. I can't wait to show you how much."

IN THE BACKYARD, JACK STOOD in front of the grill and did his best to ignore Luna as she fluttered around Max and peppered him with questions regarding Amy. In truth, Jack was uncomfortable with the line of questioning because he knew that Max was operating without all the information. In a few hours, things would be different ... but they weren't there yet.

As Max launched into some tall tale about his flirting prowess and how he finally wore Amy down enough to date him, he shifted his eyes to the tree line across the way. He loved the location of the cottage – it was quiet, relaxing, and away from prying eyes – and on most nights he and Ivy could entertain themselves for hours just sitting under the stars and staring at them. Jack filled himself with thoughts of the next night they would be able to do that and let his gaze drift. He was happily floating on a cloud of imagination ... until he caught sight of a face watching him from the foliage.

He almost gasped. At the last second, he managed to control his reaction and swallow the sound. Still, he stared at the woman standing across from him for a long time. He recognized her, but only thanks to Ivy's description. He'd never truly seen her before with his own eyes. There were times he thought he caught glimpses of her but when he took a second look he came up empty.

Until now.

Susan Bishop. The witch in the woods. Ivy met her weeks before and started learning about her magic from the long-dead woman. She was helping Ivy fill in the holes when it came to educating herself about what was happening. Jack had pretty much stayed out of that business because he didn't know what he was supposed to contribute.

Now, though, the woman was making herself visible to him. She had to have a reason.

He opened his mouth to call out to her even though he knew it would invite questions from Michael and Luna. He stopped himself when something occurred to him.

"Ivy." He turned quickly, slapping the set of tongs he carried into Luna's hands. "Watch the steaks," he muttered, his mind already somewhere else.

"What?" Luna furrowed her brow. "What's going on? Is something wrong?"

Jack didn't answer, instead barreling into the house. His gaze instantly went to the kitchen, where he expected to find her, but it was empty. Slowly, he tracked his eyes to the living room and his heart gave a terrified jolt when he saw her crumpled on the floor next to the open door.

"Son of a ... ." He ignored the murmured voices behind him and rushed to her side. Max was close behind, although his confusion was evident as he poked his head out the front door.

"I don't understand," Max said, his eyebrows drawing together. "What happened?"

"You know what I know," Jack snapped, gently sliding his hand under Ivy's head as he looked for a bump. "Honey, I need you to wake up."

Max's gaze bounced between his sister and the open door. "Where is Amy?"

Jack felt sick to his stomach as a myriad of possibilities collided in his busy brain. He already knew the answer to the question ... and yet Max was so far behind he didn't know the proper question to ask. Things were about to get ugly ... and then some.

"Max, call for an ambulance," Jack instructed as he brushed his fingers over Ivy's face. It was already puffing up and he could see the signs of a bruise forming. "She was attacked."

"Right." Max diligently pulled his phone out of his pocket. "What about Amy, though?"

Jack couldn't lie. There was no time. He needed help ... and that help was going to have to come in the form of Max. "I'm guessing that Jeff came for Amy."

"Jeff?" Max was legitimately bewildered. "I don't understand. What are you even talking about?"

Jack craned his neck when he heard footsteps in the kitchen and snagged Michael's gaze. The man was obviously confused when he walked into the scene and saw his daughter prone on the floor. "What happened?"

"That's what I'm trying to find out," Max said bitterly.

"I don't have time to explain it for everyone's benefit," Jack snapped. "Max and I have to head out if we expect to catch up to Jeff and Amy. She's in real trouble. I'll explain what's going on when we get back."

"Fair enough." Michael knelt next to Ivy. "What about her?"

"Get the paramedics here to check on her. I think she was hit in the face." The thought made Jack want to start ripping heads off random people. "You take care of her, tell her that Max and I had to go after Amy. She'll understand. She'll tell you the story."

"Who is going to tell me the story?" Max groused. "I want to know what's going on."

"I'm going to tell you." Jack was grim as he strode to the locked desk in the corner of the room and inserted a key. He had to retrieve his service weapon. "You're not going to like it. Amy wanted to tell you herself. She'll get into the nitty-gritty, but I can give you a few details."

"It must be bad if you're willing to leave Ivy when she's in this condition," Michael noted.

"It is." Jack briefly pressed his hand to his forehead and then calmed himself. "Call Brian and tell him we're in the woods and to bring backup. I'm guessing Jeff couldn't park too close to the house because he didn't want to risk being seen. We still have time. Max knows these woods like the back of his hand."

"What Jeff are you talking about?" Max demanded. "I don't know a Jeff. Unless ... you're not talking about the Jeff from the campground, are you?"

"I am." There was no easy way around this, so Jack simply blurted it out. "Jeff killed the woman at the campground. He also killed the woman here. He's Amy's husband, has terrorized her for years, and he's here to kill her. We need to make sure that doesn't happen."

Max's mouth dropped open. "You can't be serious."

"Oh, I'm serious. We're out of time to discuss it, though. We need to get after her. We can't let him leave this property with her. She won't survive if he does."

Max's expression matched his future brother-in-law's. "Then let's go. We don't have any time to waste."

Eighteen

Jack didn't want to leave Ivy, especially since she hadn't regained consciousness. He had to, though. Amy's life was on the line.

He dropped to the floor, pressed a kiss to Ivy's forehead, and moved his lips close to her ear. "I love you. I'll be back as soon as I can. You're going to be okay. I'm going to be okay, too. Susan is here. She'll lead us to Amy."

When he pulled back, he found Michael watching him with curious eyes. "Take care of her."

Once back on his feet, he jerked his head for Max to follow. "Let's go. We need to save your girlfriend."

Max was obviously still bewildered, but he nodded without hesitation. "Yeah." He waited until they were outside, until Jack was scanning the tree line for something only he could see to speak again. "Is she really married to Jeff?"

"Yes." Jack nodded at the ghost when he saw her standing on the trail. "This way." He inclined his head in that direction of the woods. "It's a long story. Ivy got it out of her this afternoon. Suffice it to say, Jeff is a bad guy and he's hurt Amy for years. She ran from him, took her son and fled when he wasn't looking one day, and has been looking over her shoulder ever since."

"Her son?" Max slowly shook his head. "I would know if she had a son."

"His name is JJ." Jack increased his pace when Susan started beckoning from in front of them. He had the feeling she was impatient, which didn't bode well for Amy. "He's five or six. I don't think she outright said how old he was. He's with Caroline right now. When Amy realized what was happening, that Jeff had followed us from the campground, she sent them away to make sure they were safe while she packed."

"Packed?" Max wanted nothing more than to slow down and absorb what Jack was telling him. There was no time for that. He recognized the urgency in Jack's movements and stayed with him even though he felt as if he was muddled in a cloud. "She was packing?"

Jack didn't have time to hold Max's hand. That didn't mean he didn't feel sorry for him. "She was afraid. She's a mother. The most important thing to her is keeping her son safe. Jeff is an abusive jerk who beat her so many times she lost count. He wants that boy ... and what sort of man do you think Jeff will create if he has a chance to mold JJ's mind?"

"But she was going to leave me, without saying goodbye."

"She was. She didn't want to, though. Once Ivy confronted her, everything spilled out. She was going to tell you all of this tonight, after your parents left. She knew you deserved the truth. She didn't want to get into everything when your parents were around to absorb it, though. I don't blame her on that front."

"I don't either. I just ... how could she keep this from me?"

Jack's patience was wearing thin. "Max, you're going to get a chance to ask her all of these questions. The thing is, we both know you're going to forgive. Once you hear her story, you're going to be angry to the point where you want to hurt someone. The someone you're going to want to hurt is the one who has your girlfriend right now, though, and I guarantee he's not going to be treating her well.

"Look what he did to your sister," he continued, his temper bubbling up. "I'm going to kill him just for that. Amy is a victim. She might not have always made the best choices, but she's trying to protect her son. She deserves kudos for that."

"I'm not saying she doesn't," Max shot back. "It's just ... I don't know how to absorb all of this. It's not what I was expecting."

"You're going to have time to absorb it. I promise you that. We need to get to Amy first, though. If he manages to get her in a vehicle and take off ... ." He left the sentence hanging because he didn't want to finish it. The possibilities were simply too horrifying.

"We have to find her." Max was firm. "Although ... how do you even know where to go?"

"You wouldn't believe me if I told you."

IVY SURFACED QUICKLY, AND WITH A VENGEANCE, back at the cottage. She jerked to a sitting position as consciousness reclaimed her and looked around with wide-eyed terror.

"Where is he?"

"Jeff?" Michael was relieved to see her awake and alert, to the point where he wanted to wrap himself around her and act as a protective shield for the foreseeable future. She was his daughter, after all. Even though she was an adult, that didn't mean he wasn't game to protect her. "He took Amy. Your brother and Jack have gone after them. I don't know what direction they're heading."

Ivy did. A familiar face showed her a vision when she was unconscious. "He parked at the nursery," Ivy volunteered, her head pounding as she rubbed her temple. "He's heading there now. You need to call Brian and have him meet us there."

"*Us?*" Michael arched an eyebrow. "We're not going over there. You were just unconscious. I have no problem telling Brian where to go to help Jack and Max, but you're officially on the sidelines of this one from here on out, young lady."

Ivy refused to play that game. "No." She struggled to her feet, swaying back and forth a bit as she regained her equilibrium. "We're going to the nursery ... and we're going to take your truck. We need to block off the exit."

"You're not going on an adventure," Michael barked. "It's not going to happen."

"Oh, it's going to happen." She patted his arm in a soothing nature. "The only question is: Are you going to help me or make me go alone?"

Michael scowled. "We're going to have a really long talk later tonight. You just wait." He scrolled through his contacts until he found Brian. "A huge talk, and you're going to be in trouble."

"Believe it or not, I'm looking forward to it."

MAX AND JACK WERE OUT of breath when they hit the nursery. Susan motioned them to move faster several times, and Jack knew better than to fight the ghost's instructions. She knew what she was doing. She'd helped them before. They needed to move faster ... so that's what they did.

By the time they cut through the center of the property, which was empty and shut down for the day, they realized they were just in time because Jeff was already in the lot, grappling with Amy as she fought him tooth and nail.

"Stop being like this," Jeff barked, grabbing a handful of hair and jerking Amy's head as far as he could.

She cried out at the sharp pain, tears filling her eyes. She didn't stop fighting, though. She knew her life depended on it. "I'm not going with you. You can't make me."

"Oh, that's where you're wrong." Jeff almost looked amused that she would dare fight with him. "I can make you do whatever I want. That's who I am. I'm pretty sure we both came to the same conclusion years ago. Unfortunately, you forgot your lessons and have to go through another tutorial. How sad is that?"

Amy's heart gave a lurch. She would rather die than go through that with Jeff again. "I'm not going." She dug her fingernails into the soft skin of his wrist, and when he hissed and readjusted his grip, she slammed the heel of her hand into his nose.

He was so surprised he released her and immediately reached for his nose, which was bleeding. "You whore! I'm going to make you pay for that!"

Amy was already scrambling back toward the woods. She was

hopeful she would be able to slip away, hide from him underneath the full bough of leaves and branches. Instead of escape, though, she found Jack and Max closing the distance.

She'd never been so happy to see anyone in her entire life.

"Max." She burst into tears as she raced toward him.

Max caught her in mid-air and brought her to him, her feet a good six inches off the ground. He kissed her forehead and cheeks as he held her tight, offering the solace she desperately needed as she buried her face in the crook of his neck.

"Hold it right there," Jack ordered, leveling his weapon on Jeff. The other man looked to be unarmed – that was his guess at least – but he wasn't taking any chances. "Put your hands up."

Jeff was incredulous when he realized he was no longer in charge of the situation. "Oh, you have to be kidding me. I should've hit that dumb broad with a brick to shut her up forever. I didn't think she would be waking up so soon; otherwise I would've killed her."

Fury he didn't know was possible for him to feel flooded Jack like an angry river of lava. "Ivy is fine." Jack believed that with his whole heart. "She's going to be fine. When I get back to her, we're going to have a long laugh about how dumb you were thinking you could get away with this in our territory."

"Your territory, huh?" Jeff arched a challenging eyebrow and shook his head. "I didn't realize you were the territorial sort, Jack. That day at the campsite, I assumed you were just some mook in love with a woman, vulnerable to her. Are you telling me you're stronger than that? Are you saying Ivy doesn't have full control over you?"

"Ivy and I are a team," Jack replied calmly as Max lowered Amy to the ground and carefully shoved her behind him so he could act as her protector. "She doesn't control me any more than I control her. Relationships are about compromise, give and take. That's what we do for each other because our relationship is the most important thing in either of our lives."

Jeff let loose a derisive snort. "Oh, what a load of crap. Relationships are about who is in power. Ask Amy. Our relationship ran much better when she acknowledged that I was the one in charge and acquiesced to my discipline."

Amy let loose a shaky sob as Max squeezed her hand. "Just go away, Jeff. I don't understand why you won't let me go. We don't belong together. We never did."

"Let you go?" Jeff rolled his eyes in a playful manner. "Why would I do that? You're my wife. We married each other forever. Besides that, you've got my son." His voice turned frigid, icy resentment practically dripping from his tongue. "I want my boy. Where is he?"

"I'm not telling you that. You can kill me and I won't tell you that."

"Care to place a wager on that?" Jeff challenged. "You will tell me before it's all said and done. I will have my boy back. He belongs with his father."

"That's not going to happen," Jack said calmly. "You're done here. You're never going to see that child again. He probably doesn't even remember you, which is a good thing. We'll make sure it stays that way."

Fury, hot and fierce, tore across Jeff's ragged features. "You will give me back my son! She took him from me. I want her arrested for custodial interference ... and stealing my property. She took money from the bank before she left, money she hid from me, that I didn't find out about until after she was already gone. She's a criminal ... and a liar."

Jack snorted, genuinely amused. Now that they had Amy back with them he wasn't in a hurry to take Jeff down. He wanted to do it in the smartest way, not the fastest way. "Sure. I would be happy to take Amy in and charge her with custodial interference. That will last exactly thirty seconds, until the prosecutor hears her story, and then she'll be free.

"You, on the other hand, are facing two murder charges," he continued. "I'm betting there might be a few other cases to pin to you before it's all said and done. We have a profile we're going to send out to police agencies in Minnesota and Michigan. Back in Idaho, we're also going to ask that they re-open the deaths of Amy's parents."

Whatever he was expecting, that wasn't it. Jeff's mouth dropped open as he worked his jaw. No sound came out, though.

"Did you think we wouldn't be able to tie those murders to you?" Jack challenged. "You weren't very smart when carrying them out. In fact, you were a blooming idiot. I still can't figure why you did it. Did you think Stacy Shepherd was Amy? Is that why you attacked her at the campground?"

"As a matter of fact, I did." Jeff smiled in such a way it made Jack's blood run cold. "I was looking for her. I saw her leave the campground. I thought she might try to disappear into the woods so I planned on following her there. I got confused, though. I saw the other woman and she was coming from the right direction ... although she was wearing a different coat. When I caught up with her, she told me to get lost, was extremely rude. I can't abide rude people. I decided to shut her up when she wouldn't stop yammering at me. I needed the quiet."

Jack merely shook his head as Amy tried to swallow her sob. "What a great specimen of the male gender you are," he muttered. "We should all try to be just like you."

"I happen to agree." Jeff made a clucking sound with his tongue. "Honestly, I felt better after doing it. I would've been angry if I killed Amy before she told me where my son was – after I would be fine with, mind you, but before is a different story – but it felt good to end Stacy."

"Is that why you went after Becky?"

"That was just dumb luck. I was driving to Shadow Lake – you two were so helpful when you told me where you lived so I didn't have to worry about following you and being caught – and I stopped at a rest area. There she was. I didn't even know she had been staying at the same campground until the news reported it. That was a coincidence."

"How lucky for Becky," Jack drawled, shaking his head.

"No one cares about Becky. No one is going to miss her. That husband of hers is better off. I know I'm much happier without a wife to drag me down. A son, on the other hand, is something to celebrate. Just give me my son and I'll go away, Amy." His tone changed as he made the offer. He almost sounded reasonable. "You'll never see me again."

"You're not going to touch him," Amy spat. "I won't ever let you near him."

"He's mine. I won't let your new boyfriend raise him. Although ...

I'm pretty sure Max didn't even know he existed." Jeff's laughter was hollow and bone-chilling. "I'm sure you'll lose him in a few hours. No one likes a lying woman, Amy. I've told you that multiple times."

"You don't know what you're talking about," Max challenged, finding his voice for the first time. "I can't wait to meet Amy's son … and he is Amy's son. You had nothing to do with raising him. I'm sure he's a bright and friendly boy because she was a wonderful mother. You're not going to have any part in his future."

"Do you want to bet?" Jeff's voice came out in a screech. "I have plans for him. He's going to be mine regardless. Just give him to me and I'll be on my way."

"That's not going to happen," Jack assured him, his weapon still clutched in his hand. "This ends here. All of it. You have two choices. You can put your hands in the air, drop to the ground and lace your fingers behind your head while I arrest you, or I'll shoot you. No other options are up for debate."

"And what if I don't want to do what you say?" Jeff shot back. "What if I want a third option?"

"You're not going to get one."

"Well, I don't happen to believe that." His eyes shone with keen interest as his fingers edged toward the back of his jeans. "I think I have one other option."

"He has a gun," Amy warned, her voice high and squeaky. "He'll shoot you. Don't let him."

Jack had no intention of letting the man draw on him. He had a fiancée waiting for him, a woman who was probably right now on her way to the hospital. He wanted to sit vigil by her bedside, be the first thing she saw when she woke up. Those were the things fueling him.

"Don't do it, Jeff," he warned. "I will put you down. I won't be sorry about it either, not even a little."

"I won't be taken alive," Jeff warned. "I have a plan. I have to stick to the plan. That's the way I operate."

"Well, then I guess we're at a stalemate. I'll be the one to end that stalemate, just so you know."

"I'm not afraid of you. In fact … ." Jeff didn't get a chance to finish what he was saying because a loud noise from the parking lot behind him drew his attention. There, a big gray truck barreled forward, seemingly coming from nowhere, and there was a furious woman behind the wheel.

Things happened in quick order. Jack barely had a chance to register that Ivy was driving her father's truck directly at Jeff before he found himself shoving Max and Amy out of the clearing and toward the trees.

"Get out of the way," he ordered at the same time Ivy plowed directly into Jeff.

She honestly wasn't going all that fast when she hit him, probably about twenty-five miles an hour. It only seemed faster because she appeared out of the blue, didn't hit her brakes, and they had no time to react.

Jeff flew about three feet in the air and then hit the ground hard. Ivy slammed the truck into park and hopped out so she could stand over him, offering Jack a wave as he breathlessly scurried to get to her.

"Is he dead?" she asked hopefully.

Jack was dumbfounded. "I don't ... what were you thinking?"

"He had a gun," Ivy replied calmly as Michael hopped out of the truck to join her. "He was going to shoot you. I couldn't let that happen."

"I had everything under control," Jack barked. "I mean ... you didn't have to run him over."

"I didn't run him over. He didn't end up under the tires at all. I ran into him. There's a difference."

"I just ... ," Jack broke off and dragged a hand through his hair before moving to Jeff to check his pulse. Oddly enough, the man was still alive. His heartbeat was steady, if a little rapid. "He's alive."

"Bummer." Ivy, her face swollen from being struck, looked sad at the prospect. "Do you think I can maybe try a second time?"

Jack couldn't stop himself from laughing even though he was determined to be stern. "Don't even think about it."

"Just one more time. I promise I'll do better."

"No."

"Please?"

"No."

"Fine." Ivy rolled her neck. "So, is anyone else hungry, or is that just me?"

Nineteen

Since Jeff was being transported to the hospital – Brian arrived just in time to ride with him – Jack insisted Ivy be checked out, too. She claimed she was fine, but he was adamant. He sat with her while Brian secured their prisoner and listened intently as the doctor laid out a list of demands regarding Ivy's care if she didn't want to spend the night in the hospital.

"She has a concussion," he warned. "We've given her a CT scan and I don't believe she has a brain bleed. You need to watch her closely, though. She needs rest and I would recommend she spend tomorrow in bed."

"Oh, I'm fine," Ivy protested, waving off the comments.

"She'll stay in bed," Jack promised. "I might even stay with her."

Once the doctor left to see about her discharge papers, Brian edged into the room and leveled his partner with a serious stare. "He's going to recover. He's not even hurt all that badly. He has two cracked ribs and, funnily enough, a concussion. He will be staying here overnight. I've already called two uniforms to watch over him. Then he'll be transported to the jail tomorrow so we can start ironing out charges."

"I guess it's good that he's alive," Jack offered. "It might be easier for Amy if he was dead, though."

"He's never going to get out of prison," Brian supplied. "He'll be locked up for life and never get access to his child. I think that's the best we can hope for in this case."

"I guess."

Brian's gaze was equally as stern when it landed on Ivy. "As for you, what were you thinking running over our suspect? Jack had everything under control and was about to take him into custody."

"He had a gun." Ivy wasn't the type to back down under normal circumstances and that was doubly true today. "Besides, he hit me in the face. Will you look at this?" She gestured toward her black eye and swollen cheekbone. "He had it coming."

"He definitely had it coming," Jack agreed. "I still don't think you should've barreled into him like that."

"It all worked out, didn't it?" Ivy stretched out on the bed. "He's alive. He'll be going to prison. Amy is okay. What more do you want from me?"

"I would like a quiet twenty-four hours," Jack replied without hesitation. "In fact, I might spend the day with you in bed tomorrow to make sure we get it."

Ivy's smile was serene. "I think that sounds like a great way to spend the day."

AN HOUR LATER, IVY WAS eager to leave the hospital. Jack had a firm hold on her arm as they hit the lobby. There, to both their surprise, Max, Michael, and Luna sat waiting for them.

"Where's Amy?" Ivy asked, instantly alert. "Did something happen to her?"

Max arched an eyebrow, his expression unreadable. "She's okay. Physically, I mean. I think it might be a while before she's okay mentally."

Ivy's heart dropped at the tone of his voice. "You didn't send her away, did you?"

"What if I did?"

"Max!" Ivy smacked him in the arm as hard as she could. "I can't believe you did that to her. I promised you were the sort of guy who stuck around. Why did you make a liar out of me?"

"Not everything is about you."

"No, but ... I really thought you would be okay with this." Ivy's heart sank. "She didn't lie out of malice, or to confuse you. She was trying to protect her son. Max, you can't hold that against her. We have no idea what she's been through. You said it yourself: It's going to take time."

Max tried to hold out – he found the disappointed look on Ivy's face to be amusing – but the bruises and swelling were enough to stop him in his tracks. "Amy and I are still together. She's out in the parking lot with Caroline and JJ. She's about to bring him in to meet us."

"Oh." Ivy was momentarily taken aback. "Well, you're an even bigger jerk because you freaked me out." She hit him again. "I knew you wouldn't just walk away, though."

Max's lips curved. "I have no intention of walking away. If you want to know the truth, now that it's all over, I actually feel better about things. Now I know why she was always holding back. Hopefully that won't be a thing moving forward."

Ivy's eyes widened as she turned them to Jack. "Didn't I tell you he would feel that way? I mean ... that's exactly what I said."

"You're beautiful and wise," Jack agreed, lifting their joined fingers so he could kiss her hand. "Now you're going to get your beautiful and wise behind home so I can take care of you. You heard the doctor. You're on bed rest for the next thirty-six hours. No exceptions."

"Oh, but ... I have work."

"I'll handle work," Michael offered. "I'm probably going to need to borrow your car, though, since my truck is going to need some body work."

Ivy pressed her lips together and averted her eyes, causing Jack to laugh and Max to shake his head.

"She saved the day," Max said finally. "I mean ... I was pretty sure Jack could take him, but it was a lot easier to just let Ivy hit him with a truck than to risk a gunfight."

"I happen to agree." Jack beamed at his fiancée. "You're still going to bed when we get home and not getting up until I say you're ready."

"You guys are absolutely no fun," Ivy lamented, her eyes moving to the front door as it opened to allow Amy entrance. She had a small boy with her. He had dark hair and eyes and looked nervous as his mother led him toward the small group. When she caught sight of Ivy, Amy let loose a long sigh of relief.

"I'm so glad you're okay," she said. "I didn't know what to think when Jeff hit you the way he did. You went over so fast ... and I was afraid he'd killed you, too."

"It turns out I have a hard head. I'm fine." Ivy hunkered down even though it caused her head to throb and leveled her gaze on the boy. "You must be JJ."

He nodded, solemn. "Yeah. How did you know that?"

"I told you, she's magical," Amy teased. "She's the reason everything is okay now, that we're okay."

"Really?" JJ didn't look convinced. "I guess you're okay. Your hair is neat."

Ivy laughed. "Thank you. That's high praise coming from you."

Slowly, JJ tracked his gaze to Max. "Who are you?"

"I'm ... your mom's friend," Max replied after a beat, dropping to his knees so he wouldn't look intimidating to JJ. "I'm hoping to be your friend, too."

JJ didn't look convinced. "Oh, yeah? What can you do that's fun?"

"Well, it's summer, so I thought we could take some trips to the lake ... and I own a lumberyard. You can visit me there. Oh, and we can go fishing. I'm an expert fisherman."

"Really?" JJ made guppy motions with his lips. "I've never been fishing before."

"I think we can make sure that's not a thing for much longer," Michael offered, grinning at the boy. "Then, in the winter, you can go sledding with Max. He's also an expert sledder."

"I am," Max agreed gravely. "No one sleds better than me."

Ivy raised her hand. "Um ... I do."

"Please." Max rolled his eyes. "I'm the one who taught you how to sled. I'm way better than you."

"That's a big load of crap," Ivy muttered, frowning. "I can't wait to beat you over the head with a sled, that's so ridiculous."

JJ laughed, the delightful sound filling the room. "Sledding sounds fun. Not as much fun as fishing, though." The last person in the group he stared at was Jack. "You're big," he said finally. "Like ... huge."

Jack chuckled. "I'm tall," he agreed. "That comes in handy when you're fishing. I think I'll go with you and Max a few times this summer, just to make sure he's teaching you the right way to do it."

"Okay." JJ seemed happy with the offer. "Do we have to stay here, though? I don't like it here."

"You mean Shadow Lake?" Amy's brow creased with concern. "I thought you liked Shadow Lake."

"Shadow Lake is cool. I meant the hospital. I was kind of hoping we could get some ice cream." The sly look JJ sent his mother told Ivy the boy knew exactly who to go to when he wanted something. That number would only grow with time.

"I think ice cream sounds fabulous," Ivy offered, stepping forward. "I'm supposed to rest, but I think a dose of ice cream first is just what the doctor ordered."

Jack started to shake his head and then darted a look toward JJ. He was resigned when he spoke. "Fine. Ice cream first. Then bed."

"Yay." JJ clapped his hands. "I love Superman ice cream," he said to Max. "Can we get that?"

"Absolutely." Max extended his hand for JJ to take and the boy slipped his much smaller hand into Max's without a moment of consideration. "Superman is my favorite, too. I think we're going to get along fine."

"I think that goes for all of us," Ivy offered, holding Amy's watery gaze. She looked happy, if a bit nervous about the new life she had in front of her. "Welcome to the family."

She meant it. Amy and JJ would be part of them now. They wouldn't want for anything, which was exactly how it was always meant to be.

Made in the USA
Las Vegas, NV
12 February 2022

43833171R00104